Motorcycle Enlightenment

Motorcycle Enlightenment

Charles Sides

HAMPTON ROADS
PUBLISHING COMPANY, INC.

Copyright © 2000
by Charles Sides

All rights reserved, including the right to reproduce this
work in any form whatsoever, without permission
in writing from the publisher, except for brief passages
in connection with a review.

Cover design by Grace Pedalino
Cover Painting by Anne Dunn

For information write:

Hampton Roads Publishing Company, Inc.
1125 Stoney Ridge Road
Charlottesville, VA 22902

Or call: 804-296-2772
FAX: 804-296-5096
e-mail: hrpc@hrpub.com
Web site: www.hrpub.com

If you are unable to order this book from your local
bookseller, you may order directly from the publisher.
Quantity discounts for organizations are available.
Call 1-800-766-8009, toll-free.

Library of Congress Catalog Card Number: 99-91420

ISBN 1-57174-172-0
10 9 8 7 6 5 4 3 2 1

Printed on acid-free paper in Canada

DEDICATION

Motorcycle Enlightenment is dedicated to my mother and father, as well as to my friend and spouse, Jenny Horner, for all her assistance and encouragement. I would also like to express appreciation to Hampton Roads Publishing Company, with special thanks to Frank DeMarco and Richard Leviton.

FOREWORD

My life had become meaningless. Every morning I got out of bed and wondered why. I ate breakfast, went to work, came home, ate dinner, watched television and slept. You might say I had become an automaton running on habits and patterns. Often times I sat and watched my children's hamster running on the wheel in his cage and surmised that he knew more about life than I did. At least he seemed to enjoy running.

In the background someone or something kept calling me, kept pulling me on, when all I wanted to do was disappear. For a long time I ignored this voice, but one day it spoke loudly with a not-so-gentle tone. It got my attention and I began to listen.

I realized that in addition to being exhausted, I was unhappy, lonely and confused. My life and the world in general made no sense. So I began a frantic search to find the answer. In a way I got off one treadmill and onto another. I voraciously read everything I could find on philosophy, psychology and religion. I performed self-help exercises in order to find my inner being, fragmented being, lost being and nonexistent being. I walked, jogged and sprinted. I meditated, chanted and sang. I discovered that, "I am God" and "God is dead." And then, somewhere along the journey, I started *being*. And that has made all the difference.

1.

I always thought I'd write a book that began with the words "It was the worst of times" because I thought they perfectly reflected my life. I wrote them on the back of a business card and carried them with me for ten years. I knew that as long as they were safely tucked inside my wallet it would be fulfilled. The story goes like this:

I lived a paradox in which I thought I had everything that would make me happy but knew that nothing I had was actually making me happy. My life consisted of a wife, two children, two businesses, two houses, three cars, a motorcycle, three computers, three televisions, and two VCRs, but little happiness. No matter what I did, happiness escaped my grasp.

So, at the end of every business day, I headed home exhausted, depressed and lost. Often I was literally lost, but that's another chapter. Something was missing in my life but I didn't know what it was. Did I *need* another car? A Corvette or Jaguar would be nice. I often pictured myself speeding through life, outrunning even my own thoughts. But I digress already. The point is, or was, that when I lay down at night and closed my eyes, I asked aloud, "Who am I? Why am I here? What is the purpose of life?"

Motorcycle Enlightenment

There was no one I could talk to about these questions, and my wife Sheila had given up trying years ago. She and I would be sitting on the couch watching television and eating snacks when I'd sigh and say, "What's the purpose of all this?"

Sheila would turn off the television, look forlornly at me and say, "For the zillionth time, I don't know. I don't question life. I love my children. I love my job. I love most of my life." When she said "most of my life," I should have seen the writing on the wall and realized I was on the wrong side of "most," but I was too involved in reading about Egyptian hieroglyphics.

My inability to have a meaningful existence manifested itself in dissatisfaction with life in general, but, more specifically, in my vocation. (I think that sentence came from a self-help book.) What it means is that I had had a lot of jobs, but since I had been self-employed, I had fired myself.

Skipping a few details, suffice it to say that one day after twenty years of marriage, Sheila calmly said, "I'd like you to leave. Go find your happiness. It's not here."

Two days later I was staying in a motel, two weeks later in my own apartment. When the assets and liabilities were decided, the divorce was final. In one of my fits of inspiration or insanity, (they often resemble each other and I get them confused), I decided to sell almost all of my possessions, except the motorcycle. By shedding my entanglements, I thought I'd be free to search for the elusive meaning of life, i.e., happiness. I knew the answer was out there waiting to be found.

I fantasized about riding my cycle to California and mile by mile becoming enlightened to the truths of the world. Yes, in my ecstatic moments, I saw myself as

America's savior. I was making this journey not only for myself but also for every unhappy being in the world, for every individual who hated his job and for the downtrodden and humbled masses. "America, I hear you calling and I'm on my way."

In my depressed moments, I knew I was running away. I had no idea where I was running to, but that didn't matter. Running just felt very good.

Only two negatives stood in my way. The first was that I got terrible leg cramps after riding my motorcycle for as little as fifteen minutes. The second was that I have no sense of direction. For most of my life I lived in a town with a population of three thousand people and one traffic light. Still, I kept a map on the front seat of my car.

To give you a better idea of how bad my sense of direction is, many years ago when my children were young, they made me a papier-mâché arrow. (They had learned that their father was usually lost, especially when he pulled off the road into a gas station or restaurant.) So they suggested I place the arrow on the dashboard of the car pointing in the direction I'm headed. It worked.

When I'm at shopping malls I count spaces, lines of cars, and light poles, and often draw a map of the mall so I can retrace my steps and find the car. Hansel and Gretel are my idols.

2.

As I finish last minute preparations I wonder if anyone needs to know that I'll be leaving in the morning. My Franklin Planner (an unused Christmas present) isn't much help. There's nothing scheduled for the entire year except a dental appointment in October. I'm not exactly a socialite. I make a list of chores to be completed: 1. Call dentist. 2. Get gas for cycle.

After that task is completed I lie down on the floor of my now bare apartment, listen to music, and try to sleep. Thoughts go through my head continuously until there's one that eventually seems useful. I roll over, pick up the notepad lying beside me and add number 3. to the list: Call auto club for directions.

In spite of my anxiety, I sleep through the night and awake knowing that today is the day. Optimistically, I know that in several hours I'll be part way to California. Pessimistically, I know that in several hours I'll be very sore from riding my motorcycle part way to California.

I get up, shower and dress quickly. The note lying on the floor reminds me to call the dentist and cancel the appointment. I've never done that before. Dentists are so authoritarian. But it's very easy and finished within minutes. The manic side of my personality bursts forth as I yell to the apartment walls, "Free at last. Free at last. Thank God Almighty, I am free at last."

Feeling self-conscious, I realize that was a little much. Rationalizing, I decide that it's okay because I'm afraid of dentists and flinch whenever the hygienist gets within a foot of my chair. Besides, they refuse to give me general anesthesia when cleaning my teeth.

So, having confronted the dental profession, I feel courage rising within me. This propels me on to item 3. on the note. Call the auto club for directions, not to California, to the auto club. First things first. The conversation doesn't go as smoothly as the one with the dental office. The receptionist at the auto club doesn't understand that I only want directions to the auto club. "When I get there," I explain to her, "you can give me directions to California."

I carefully write down her instructions and take them out to the motorcycle. Where do I put the directions so I can check them as I ride? A flash of insight tells me to get masking tape at the apartment rental office so I can affix them to the—I can never think of the name of that dial, the one that shows RPMs. I never use it anyway. Actually, I don't know what it's for, so I follow my impulse and tape the directions on it.

The motorcycle is packed with my few remaining possessions. I get on and I'm off to find America. But first I must find the auto club. The AAA sign is right where the receptionist said it would be and I pull into the parking lot. Balancing the cycle carefully, I try to pull it up onto the stand, but it's too heavy. The kickstand is facing uphill so I can't use it. I back out of the space, turn around and back in. This time the kickstand is aiming downhill and seems to hold the weight of the cycle. I

Motorcycle Enlightenment

carefully get off, lock my helmet under the seat, and go inside.

After taking a number I fidget nervously and look at it every few seconds. Annoyed with myself I finally stick it in my pocket and sit down. About ten minutes later, when number 47 is called, I say "That's me" a little too loudly and walk to the counter.

"May I have the number please?"

"Sure. It's right . . . ah . . . ." I reach into my pocket and can't find it. Now I panic and search every pocket. But, the more nervous I get, the more I know I'll never find it. "I can't find it."

"You lost the number?" the clerk asks incredulously.

"Number 47," he calls again. No one responds.

"Okay, go ahead. It must be you."

"Must be."

Instantly, I know not to tell him that I'm searching for America and enlightenment. With a moment's deliberation I say, "I'm heading for California. May I have directions?"

He turns to get maps.

Safe, I think. Even though I lost my number, I handled that part okay.

"Where in California?"

Panic! I hadn't thought about that. "Los Angeles," I decide quickly.

"Nice place. My brother lives there."

"I'll tell him you said hello if I see him."

He just looks at me.

Too much, I remind myself. Relax.

He lays out a map of the United States and highlights lines. "Take Route 30 to 83 to the PA Turnpike. Follow the Turnpike to Route 70. Take Route 70 the whole way to Utah. Then 15 and 10 to Los Angeles."

"That's it? I won't even have to tape that on the tachometer. Tachometer!" I say with great enthusiasm. "That's the name of the dial I couldn't think of earlier."

He waits patiently.

"Thanks," I say and leave.

As I walk away I hear him call number 48. Instinctively I reach into my pocket to check if that's my number and pull out number 47. Where had it been? I turn back towards the counter to show him I really did have the number, but second thoughts intervene. Somehow I don't think he cares. I put the number back in my pocket and walk outside. The cycle is still standing. Things are looking good.

With directions in hand, my ego swells and I swagger the final few steps to the cycle. I put on the helmet, throw my leg over the seat, kick the bag tied on the back and catch myself before falling. Ego safely in check, I step across the seat and begin my mental program. Insert key, turn on gas, turn on cycle and make sure the handlebar switch is in the "on" position. (I once spent a half-hour trying to start the cycle with the switch in the "off" position.)

Feeling some bravado, I decide to kickstart the cycle instead of using the electric starter. I flip the top of the crank outward, jump a little higher than necessary and kick away. Unfortunately I forget the cycle is on the slant and my right leg can't reach the ground. I almost fall over.

The electric starter works and I drive away. At the first stop sign I reach into my pocket, take out the checklist and mentally cross out what I've done. Call dentist: done. Stop at auto club: done. Get gas: next. I head for the gas station with trepidation. Sometimes the key for

Motorcycle Enlightenment

the gas cap doesn't work and I can't get the tank open. I start to worry.

As I pull into the station, I notice there are no other cars at the pumps so I'm relieved. I hate to look stupid in front of others. I turn off the engine and put the key in the gas cap. Presto. It opens. After carefully filling the tank without spilling a drop, I put the hose back. A car pulls in. Then another. Now the gas cap won't go on. I try again. I look to see if the two little metal prongs on the cap are lined up with the tank. They are. I put the cap on the tank and pound. One driver looks over and smiles. The other says, "Having trouble?"

I roll my eyes and answer, "Yeah. Can't get the cap on."

He walks over, looks at the cap for a moment, lines up the prongs, and pushes it right into place. "Maybe the prongs weren't lined up."

They were, I grumble to myself.

"Thanks," I say to him.

I pay for the gas, use the electric starter, and pull out into traffic. A thought flashes through my mind. I wonder how I get to Route 30. I could go back to the auto club and ask. I still have number 47. I'll ask when I get lunch. Everybody knows where Route 30 is.

Automatically I reach back to feel if my wallet is still there. It is. This is a habit I developed some time ago and continue reinforcing every time I check. I thought about buying a wallet with a chain that clipped, buckled or stapled to the belt loop on my pants. But I know I'd check to see if the wallet, chain and belt loop were still there.

I look at my watch and discover it's only 11:15 A.M. Somehow I thought the days, actually this first day of freedom, would go faster. But it's dragging on. I decide to have an early lunch before heading to California, figuring that still leaves time for six hours riding and twenty-four leg cramps. The next major decision is where to eat. Pizza sounds good but I can hear my mother saying, "You should have some vegetables. You'll get scurvy." But I'm free now, so I can get scurvy if I want.

At the local pizza shop the hostess greets me and asks, "Smoking or nonsmoking?"

"Nonsmoking, and as far from smoking as possible," I reply. She walks to a table, picks up a dirty ashtray and says, "This is nonsmoking."

I must attract these situations to myself. Over the years I've learned that nonsmoking tables are the empty ones. There are no other requirements. I order the "ten minute special or it's free" which arrives in fifteen minutes. No one seems concerned and I don't have the courage to ask for a free meal. The food's okay and I tip well even though the waitress never appeared again. At the cash register I ask for directions to Route 30. A young man nonchalantly rattles off some road names, which I desperately try to remember. I'm already thinking that I'll stop at the next corner and ask someone else.

Outside I look for my car and remember that I sold it. I only have the motorcycle. But thoughts of California bring a smile to my face. I tape the directions from the auto club on the left side of the tachometer so I can still see the red line on the right. Even though I don't know exactly what happens if the needle touches the red, I know it shouldn't, which means I need to watch it. Besides, it gives me one more thing to do besides checking for my wallet.

I check for my wallet. Next I must find someone who knows where Route 30 is. I glance up and see a "To 30" sign at the corner and consider it a good omen. This is it. I'm off.

My left leg cramps so I know I've ridden fifteen minutes. Flashes of having been on this road before make me wonder if I'm going the right way. I should know Route 30, I keep telling myself. Then it hits me. Of course, Route 30 is the "big road." I designate roads according to "big, little, ends up at the bridge, goes to the gas station, takes me to work." If I'm not on one of these roads, I drive aimlessly. This used to drive Sheila crazy. At intersections she would watch to see if I put on the turn signal. When I didn't she would ask, "Do you know where you're going?"

"No," I would answer.

"Then how do you plan to get there?"

"I don't know that either," I would respond.

"Alan," she would say with exasperation. "If you don't know where you're going, how can you get there?"

That was always a tough question. I never had an answer.

Nevertheless, here I am on Route 30 heading . . . east, according to a sign I just passed. California is definitely west. Even I know something's wrong. I take the first exit and pull into a convenience store. With my helmet still on I go into the store and ask the clerk for directions to the PA Turnpike. She looks at me strangely so I take off the helmet and try again.

"May I have directions to the PA Turnpike?"

"Route 30 to 83," she says.

"East or west on Route 30?"

"West."

"Darn."

"Pardon?"

"Nothing."

I hesitate a moment, then ask, "How far am I from the Turnpike?"

"About an hour," she answers.

Four cramps, I think.

An idea flashes through my mind. I'm on 30 East and I know that's the way to New Jersey. Maybe I should go to Ocean City first and get used to riding the cycle. Then I could go to California. I know my way around the shore. Sheila used to say, "How could you get lost on the boardwalk? It only runs north and south." All I know is the water's on one side and the town's on the other. I hardly ever get them mixed up.

I ask the clerk if she knows the directions to Ocean City, New Jersey.

"30 East to 41 South to 40 East and then follow the signs."

I grab a napkin from the hot dog and coke display, borrow the pen on the counter and write down the directions before I forget them. I thank her and leave.

Back at the cycle I peel off the old directions and replace them with "30E 41S 40E." The directions don't look that difficult. I know if I wasn't thinking a thousand other thoughts, I could remember them without any trouble. Why do I think so much? I decide to think more about that later.

Now to get back on 30 East. Panic. Which way was I going? I nervously glance up and see a sign about twenty feet to my right. "Route 30 East." I pull out.

"New Jersey" and "Yikes" I say aloud. I have to cross the Delaware Memorial Bridge. I start to worry about that at the same time I check to see if my wallet is there.

Motorcycle Enlightenment

It's early afternoon and I relax into the riding. In fact, I enjoy myself. I've driven to the shore at least fifty times, never by myself, and never on a motorcycle. The shore all by myself for the first time: this could be fun.

Cramps come and go as the time slips by. The scenery looks vaguely familiar, but I confess I have no idea where I am or how far I have to go.

Suddenly I come around a turn and spot the twin towers of the Delaware Memorial Bridge. My heart beats faster. I start up the bridge. I look straight ahead and realize I have no idea where I'm going in life. I look to my right and see nothing but sky and water. A strong wind could suddenly blow the cycle and me over the side. Meaningless life before me and possible death beside me. What a choice. I keep riding.

Another thought flashes. Maybe this odyssey isn't so much a trip of freedom as it is a chance to free me from myself. I don't know exactly what that means, but it deserves some later thought. I add it to the list.

I arrive at the top of the span and head for the far right lane which feels safer, although there isn't anything solid between the water and me. I don't think I really want to die. I keep my eyes straight ahead and breathe easier when I'm almost across. Forty feet, ten feet, safe. Thank goodness. I wonder if I have to cross any bridges on the way to California. Maybe I'll just stay in New Jersey the rest of my life.

As I get closer to Ocean City I begin to relax a little. At times I can almost remember some of the route. At one point it occurs to me that I haven't had a cramp for awhile. A few times I think I'm not thinking. I'm simply enjoying the scenery and the ride. This is definitely out of character, but it feels good.

Suddenly I know I have to take a right turn ahead. I'm amazed I know that. Sure enough, there's a sign for Ocean City. After the turn I know I'm getting close because the scenery starts to look more like the shore. Here's where I begin to get excited. I enjoy riding a bicycle on the boardwalk, eating doughnuts with sugar sprinkles, walking on the beach, eating pizza and watching people. The anticipation is growing. A few more miles to go.

3.

Unbelievable! There's the water tower so I'm officially in Ocean City. I'm as excited as if I had just arrived in California because I drove somewhere all by myself and didn't get lost. Since I changed my mind about going to California, this doesn't count as being lost. So after I made up my mind that this was where I was heading, it counts that I got here.

It's late afternoon, almost dinner time, and I know where I want to eat: Angelo's Pizza. I park the cycle on a back street, lock my helmet under the seat, and stand up. Oh, the pain! My rear end's asleep, my legs are numb, and the motorcycle is still roaring in my ears. Maybe I'll fly to California.

I hear waves breaking on the beach. I love that sound. I walk up the boardwalk ramp, over to the railing and look out across that wise, wonderful ocean. I wonder if a woman in France is staring back at me from across the ocean. I have no idea if France is directly across the ocean from New Jersey. At age sixteen I decided it was and never looked at the globe. It would have ruined the mystique.

I turn around, spot Angelo's Pizza and think to myself: the ocean on one side, pizza on the other. Is this heaven or what?

I walk into the restaurant and take my usual seat facing the back wall. It's a habit. When Sheila and I used to come here, she liked to look at the ocean so I always gave her the better seat. But since I'm alone now, I get up and sit down on the other side of the table. No wonder she liked sitting here. It's a much better view than the Pepsi clock. I order and eat two slices. Sometimes the memory of a food is better than its actual taste, but not this time.

I fantasize that I could eat and sleep here at the table, but I know better. The thought of finding a place to stay drags me out of the restaurant and back to the cycle. A sigh of relief escapes me when I see my bag still strapped to the luggage rack. I tenderly return to the cycle seat and drive aimlessly looking for an apartment to rent. On my left I spot a real estate agency and pull into the parking lot.

An agent greets me when I walk into the office and offers me a chair beside her desk.

"Hello. My name is Jean."

"Hi. I'm Alan."

"How may I help you?"

"I'm looking for a place to stay for a few weeks, a month or maybe forever."

"How many people are in your party?"

"Just me, no party. I'm on my way to California."

She smiles. "California? That's on the other coast."

"I know, but this is on the way for me."

"Okay," she says and smiles.

Jean swings her chair towards the computer and begins searching for available apartments. Meanwhile, thoughts run through my mind. She's attractive. I wonder if she's married. I wonder if I'll get married again. What am I doing in New Jersey?

Motorcycle Enlightenment

"Would you please fill out this application?" she asks.

"Yes," I say, beginning to worry that I have neither a job nor a permanent address. I'm no longer the owner of two businesses. I'm a biker, although I don't fit the stereotype decked out in unassuming sneakers, jeans and windbreaker.

As I'm filling out the papers Jean asks a question. "Would you be interested in a two-bedroom apartment or is that too large?" Before I can answer, she adds an explanation. "A friend of mine has a duplex but she's particular about who rents it. She doesn't even list the property. Often it goes unrented all summer but I could call her."

"Fine. I'd like to see it."

Jean calls the woman and asks if she may show the house. The woman agrees. As we stand up to leave I look at the nameplate on the desk: "Jean Vaness." That's easy. At least I can remember Jean, if my mind isn't cluttered with other thoughts.

Jean and I walk out to the car. I get in and sit down gingerly. This makes her smile and even laugh a little.

"Sore?" she asks.

"It was a long ride."

On the way Jean fills me in on the type of person I need to be if I want to rent the apartment. It turns out I am that person. I don't drink, smoke, stay up late, or have any bad habits, other than thinking too much. That couldn't be a problem. Besides, how would she know unless I told her?

"Who owns the apartment?" I ask.

"Alice Crawley, a very good friend of mine."

"You mentioned that she doesn't rent the apartment all the time? Why not?" My business mind is always functioning.

"She doesn't need to. She and her husband Stuart used to own this real estate agency, but Alice sold it after he died. She's quite wealthy."

"Must be nice."

Jean looks at me strangely but doesn't say anything.

"How old was her husband when he died?"

"Fifty-seven," Jean says. "One night he went to bed and had a massive heart attack. I miss him. He was someone special."

"I'm sorry," I respond to her. He's lucky, I think to myself. "What's Mrs. Crawley like?"

"Oh, you'll like her. She's a sweet person."

We pull up in front of the house and Jean waves to Alice who is sitting on the porch waiting. We get out of the car and start up the sidewalk, but Jean stops. Bending down she gently touches a flower and smells its fragrance. "Alice, these are so lovely."

I pause too, glance at the flowers, and continue walking.

Jean introduces me. "Alice" she says, "this is Alan Pierce. Alan, Alice Crawley."

Alice reaches out and shakes my hand. "It's nice to meet you, Alan."

"Thank you, Mrs. Crawley. It's nice meeting you too. Thank you for letting me look at your house. It's charming."

She smiles and at the same time I sense I'm getting a once-over, twice-over, and thrice-over.

"So, what brings you to New Jersey?" she asks.

"A terrible sense of direction," I answer truthfully.

"He's on his way to California," Jean adds.

"The long way," I explain.

Mrs. Crawley, seeming to want more substantial information inquires, "May I ask your occupation?"

Motorcycle Enlightenment

"I'm a businessman," I reply, then add, "but I don't own any businesses right now. I'm an in-between-business businessman."

She smiles. Jean smiles. I smile. I think I'm in.

Mrs. Crawley hands Jean the key and suggests that we look at the apartment. Jean unlocks the door, gestures for me to go in, and follows me. The living room is nicely furnished and includes a television and VCR. Off to the right is an eat-in kitchen, and to the left is a half-bath. The second floor has two bedrooms and a bathroom. It's perfect. At seven hundred dollars per month, I can afford to live here for a year and not have to work. California is already becoming a distant memory.

We go back to Mrs. Crawley and tell her I'd like to rent the apartment. I assure her I don't drink, smoke, or even swear. I'm loyal, kind, obedient and trustworthy, although I quit the Boy Scouts after a week of knot-tying and one hike.

Without checking my references, Mrs. Crawley agrees to rent me the apartment and says that I may sign an open lease that requires only a thirty-day termination notice. That means, to me, I may stay a month, a year, or the rest of my life.

I inform Mrs. Crawley that I'll be returning on a motorcycle but not to worry. She'll never find me working on it in the driveway because I have no idea how to take it apart or put it back together. In fact, if I put the key in the ignition and it doesn't start, I don't know what to do. At that point I would have already exhausted my mechanical knowledge. I also tell her that I won't be riding it for some time because parts of my anatomy will be recovering for weeks.

How did I think I could ride to California? I wonder silently.

Jean and I walk back to the car.

"Alice likes you," she says.

"Really? How can you tell?"

"Just a feeling."

We return to the office and go inside to sign the lease agreement. When the paperwork is completed, she hands me a key and says, "It was nice meeting you, Alan. I hope you enjoy your stay in Ocean City."

"Thanks," I reply. "I'm sure I will, and I really do appreciate your help." I stand up to leave and then sense a mild panic "Oh my," I say. "I almost forgot. Would you please draw a map so I can find the house again? I'm not..."

". . . good with directions," she says, finishing my sentence. Jean draws a detailed map with a huge star where the house is located.

I thank her and start to leave. After a few steps towards the door Jean's voice catches my attention and I look back.

"I'll check on you tomorrow," she says.

"You will?"

"Just to make sure you're okay," she adds.

I nod and leave.

I tape Jean's directions on the tachometer and follow them back to the house, making only two wrong turns. Back at Mrs. Crawley's I park the motorcycle behind the garage and empty the saddlebags. Carrying everything I own in one trip gives me a sense of freedom.

Upstairs in the bedroom I unpack a bag of underwear, socks, handkerchiefs, pants, and shirts. In another bag are books, a Walkman, and some audio and video tapes. I take out the notebook and pens with which I had planned to write a book about my trip to California. Now the first page will read, "Well, here I am in New Jersey."

Motorcycle Enlightenment

I decide to eat again so I walk downtown and look for a familiar restaurant, but everything looks different. When Sheila and I were together, I used to point out new stores and restaurants, only to have her impatiently say, "That's been here at least ten years."

"See," I'd say, "The world always looks new and different to me."

"You just don't pay attention," she would respond and walk on.

I select a restaurant and order a normal meal, one that has vegetables. After eating, I walk up on the boardwalk and stroll along with the crowd. I try to imagine what people are thinking. Are they happy? Are they confused? Do they even know they're here, or are they lost in thoughts of the past or future?

I wonder all the time what life is about. I stop walking, lean on the railing, and look at the ocean. What is the meaning of life? Why do things happen the way they do? One person says "Dumb luck." But dumb luck doesn't seem right to me. Another says, "Only God knows." But if there's an all-knowing, loving God who creates this world, why does he make sick, deformed babies? Why was I born to a middle class family in the United States while another child was born with leprosy in a third-world country? I wonder if the French woman across the water is driving herself crazy with similar thoughts.

But there are answers and, somehow, I know I'm going to find them. I don't know where, how, or when, but I know that one day, the light will go on. I stand gazing at the ocean for an hour and listen to the waves breaking on the sand.

I turn to see the people walking and shopping but the

pizza sign attracts my attention. I'll drown my thoughts in pizza for the third time today. But at least I had vegetables for dinner. What is scurvy anyway?

I walk back to Mrs. Crawley's. It isn't that late and her lights are still on. I unlock my door, head straight for the bedroom, flop down on the bed, look up at the ceiling, and say out loud, "Here's this body. I have no idea what I'm doing here or how I fit into the great scheme of things, but I'd sure like some answers. Will someone please help me?"

I wake up at two A.M., look around the room and wonder where I am. Neither the flowered curtains nor the white cane furniture look familiar. Then I remember: Ocean City.

I get up, put on pajamas and return to bed. I realize there isn't anything I have to do in the morning. This freedom thing has its ups and downs. I used to work long hours in my accounting firm and doing the books for my retail store. I didn't enjoy it, but at least I knew what I was doing. Numbers and spreadsheets make sense. They're logical and reliable. I wish life were like this. Maybe I should try finding a business at the shore. Here's the beginning of the thinking cycle. To stop the next thought before it starts, I grab my Walkman and push play.

Around nine A.M. I wake up disoriented as usual. At least I don't panic as much as I used to. I just look around until I see something familiar or a memory floats in. Sometimes acclimating to my surroundings seems to take forever, but that's probably an exaggeration. Ocean City? From somewhere I think I hear, "That's right."

A flurry of thoughts—ocean, boardwalk, doughnuts. I shower quickly and head for 13th Street where bicycles can be rented. I choose a three-speed with a basket,

Motorcycle Enlightenment

essential for carrying doughnuts, and hop on, forgetting that a bicycle and a motorcycle have the same type of seat, and forgetting my rear end is sore.

I ride up the ramp, across the boardwalk, and stay as close to the rail as possible. Walkers pass me as if I'm standing still. I look down to see if the tire has stopped, but it's still going around. Therefore I must be moving forward. Verses of songs fill my mind. I get inspired and want to change the world, invent things, start businesses. And then I disappear. For an instant or two, there's no one riding the bicycle; there's no boardwalk and no ocean. Just here. This happens when I play tennis and watch movies. I lose that separation and become the activity. I think my thoughts stop or at least flow beneath conscious level. What a relief.

I'm back now. My sense of smell is terrible and I cannot identify one fragrance from another. But I know when there's a scent in the air that's different from what was there before. Unfortunately, it might be a skunk or a flower. I can't tell. I know something is different. I look around to see what it is and, to my surprise, it's the doughnut shop. I buy three doughnuts, one with red sprinkles, one with brown and one with orange. I also get some milk and put these treasures into the basket. I ride the length of the boardwalk, stop, and sit down on the bench. Off in the distance, Atlantic City is partly shrouded in fog and looks like a mirage floating in the air.

The doughnuts are delicious. Somehow I don't think they make a good breakfast, but I won't do this everyday. Today I'm on vacation. Vacation from what? I don't have a job. I'll worry about that tomorrow. "Today is the first day of the rest of my life." All right, but so was yesterday and the day before that. I haven't done well with first days. Maybe if I skip to second days, things would be different. I think my problem has to do with the pressure of starting over each day.

I turn my bike around and ride back closer to the shops and look in the windows. Eventually, I come to 13th Street. I like Ocean City. I start out on 13th Street, and ride to the far end, turn around, and ride back to 13th Street. Sometimes I ride to the other end and back too. But I never get lost. The ocean is on one side and stores are on the other. Life should be this simple.

I return my bicycle and ask the attendant if he knows where the telephone company is. He does and gives me directions. I borrow his pencil and jot them down on my receipt while he repeats them. On paper they look easy.

I follow the directions carefully, walk inside the phone office and tell the receptionist that I'd like to have a telephone installed. She hands me a form to complete. Luckily I picked up a business card at Mrs. Crawley's so I know the address. I hesitate where it says occupation and write "on vacation." The receptionist takes the form when I finish, makes a call, and gives me a date and time. I nod, she says okay, and it's done.

I try to follow the directions in reverse and take a few wrong turns. Since I've been here, I've done nothing but sleep and eat, which isn't unusual, except that I haven't worked in between.

I decide that I can't eat every meal at a restaurant, so I walk downtown to purchase a microwave. I walk into the store, buy one and carry it home. (That's the first time I thought of Mrs. Crawley's as home.) With a twinge of sadness, I realize I can't carry everything I own on the motorcycle anymore.

Motorcycle Enlightenment

Next stop is the grocery store. I walk there too. A car is starting to sound like a good idea. I buy five TV dinners, five chicken pies, five beef pies, frozen french fries, ice cream and Cool Whip. I walk home and load my freezer. For lunch I have a beef pie, ice cream and Cool Whip. I feel pleased with myself.

Only one P.M., I never knew days could be so long. I go upstairs and lie down to take a nap. I'm not tired now, but when I worked ten-hour days I was. Therefore, this is retroactive sleep, and I rationalize myself into resting comfortably.

A knock at the door startles me. I sit up. Where am I? Who could be knocking? Where's the door? I slowly get reoriented and head down the steps to open the front door. Jean is already heading back to her car.

"Wait," I yell.

She turns, "Oh, I didn't think you were here."

"I didn't know where the door was."

"What?"

"Uh, I was upstairs and couldn't get to the door fast enough," I correct myself. "So did you really stop to check on me?"

"I said I would," she reminds me.

"You're very thoughtful. I don't know anyone else who would do that."

"Really?" She looks surprised. "You seem like a nice guy."

"I am," I assure her. "Only it seems to be a secret nobody knows."

"Well, I hope you'll let me in on it."

Sure, I think to myself. To her I say, "I will. How can I do that?"

"You could go out to dinner with me tonight?"

"Really? Dinner with you? Why would you want to do that?"

She looks puzzled.

Quickly I say, "Yes, that would be fine."

"Great. What time?" she asks.

"Seven?"

"Okay. I'll pick you up unless you want to ride the motorcycle."

"Riding in a car sounds wonderful," I assure her.

Jean smiles and walks to her car. After she gets in, she looks back and waves. I watch her drive away. The realization of what just occurred sinks in. I'm going out to dinner with Jean tonight. I add a question to my list: Who am I? Why am I here? What's the purpose of all this? Why does Jean want to go out with me? These are questions that shake the universe.

I walk back inside and look at the clock: 3:45 P.M. About three hours to go. I better start getting ready.

I'm punctual. Maybe that's why there was so much pressure with dental appointments. I would paper-clip the dentist's business card to my calendar and prepare for the appointment the whole month. Whenever I looked at the calendar, I automatically played the coming scene in my mind. I play every scene many times in my mind before it takes place. Tonight with Jean will be no exception.

I'm dressed and ready to go, but it's only 4:15 P.M. To fill the time I walk to the store, buy the Ocean City paper and turn to the business opportunity section. Although I have no idea what I want to do, I look anyway. Nothing looks interesting so I walk home slowly, stretch out on the couch and read the rest of the paper. It's short and doesn't take even a half-hour to finish.

Motorcycle Enlightenment

5:15 P.M. I'm not sure I ever looked at the clock more times than today. If an hour's this long, what's eternity like? I go upstairs, look in the mirror again to see if I'm dressed okay, and comb what little hair I have. I hear a knock, and this time I know where the door is and head downstairs.

Expecting Jean, I must show surprise when I see Mrs. Crawley.

"Sorry to disappoint you, Alan," she says.

"Oh, not at all," I lie. "How are you?"

"I'm fine," she answers. "Jean's on the phone and wants to know if she can come early. She finished her work."

"Sure," I respond eagerly.

"So you two are going out tonight?"

"Yes, I think Jean feels sorry for me."

"I think there's more to it than that," Mrs. Crawley says as she walks away. "I'll tell her you're waiting anxiously."

"Don't make me sound too anxious," I add, but it's too late.

4.

Jean pulls up about fifteen minutes later. I watch from the upstairs window and wait until she knocks on the door. I look in the mirror for the twentieth time, run my hand over my head to see if any hair has grown, and go downstairs. Opening the door I try to be calm and say, "Hello again."

"Hi," she says. "I'm glad you could be ready earlier. My last appointment canceled. I hope it's not an inconvenience."

How could I tell her there's nothing I have to do or want to do in the world? To Jean I say, "No, I could have been ready for dinner this morning."

"Really? Well, I guess it's difficult being in a town where you don't know anyone, especially if you don't have a job."

"I'm used to not knowing anyone but not working is a little different."

She doesn't question my response.

"Thank you for asking me out," I say. "This is very kind."

"My pleasure. I have to tell you I was intrigued by your comment that New Jersey is on the way to California."

"That's a long story. It could take several dinners."

I mean this innocently but realize it has other implications.

"I suppose we'll have to take one dinner at a time," she responds.

I consider the comment and decide that she means we'll have to see how this evening goes before we plan another. My heart sinks. It's been over a year since my divorce, and just thinking about being with Jean this evening made me realize how lonely I've been. Part of me wants another relationship; part of me doesn't. I'm flattered that Jean wants to spend an evening with me, but instantly worried she might not want to spend every evening with me. I try to relax and realize I should be glad to have *this* evening. I'll worry about tomorrow evening tomorrow.

We get into the car but I must look uncomfortable.

"Is something the matter?"

"No, not really. This is just very different for me. It's been almost thirty years since I've had a . . ."

"Date?"

"Yeah . . . date . . . with anyone. I don't remember how to act."

She touches my arm. "We'll call this a business dinner."

"Okay," I agree. "I suppose realtors can take clients out."

"Certainly. It's in the contract."

Neither of us talks for a few minutes, but the silence unnerves me. "So where are we going?"

"To my favorite restaurant," Jean says. "I reserved a table near the water where we can sit and talk until they close."

I relax a little more. "I can't believe this."

"Believe what?" she asks.

"That I'm sitting here in this car with you."

She laughs and reminds me, "We're just going out for dinner. People do that, you know."

"Not me," I assure her.

We pull into the parking lot and I remember this restaurant. "For all the times I've been in Ocean City, I never ate here, even though I always thought it looked interesting."

Jean ventures a guess. "Were you going to California to escape something but changed your mind and headed for familiar territory instead?"

"I'm not a criminal if that's what you mean."

"No," she laughs, "I didn't mean that."

"Then yes, in a way, you're right. My life has fallen apart."

"I could guess from your eyes," she says. "They tell a lot about you."

"Do they tell you I'm extremely nervous right now?"

She looks surprised. "No, I wouldn't have guessed that. Outwardly you seem confident."

"Inwardly, I'm worrying whether the restaurant is fancy and if I'll know which fork to use. That fear, along with dropping something on my beige pants, is dominating my thoughts."

Jean smiles. "Relax. It's not fancy and I won't laugh if you drop your food."

"Promise?"

"Promise," she says.

"Are you doing this because you feel sorry for me?"

"No," she answers.

"Is it because I'm bald?"

"Absolutely."

Motorcycle Enlightenment

The hostess seats us at the best table in the restaurant, which is actually outside on a deck overlooking the bay. I close my eyes and listen to the water caressing the dock. Seagulls call to one another across the bay. I realize that I'm safe in New Jersey, have a pleasant apartment, and enough money to live for a year without working. I open my eyes and see a beautiful woman sitting in front of me. "I think I'm in heaven," I tell her. "I probably died driving my motorcycle across the Delaware Memorial Bridge and this is where I'll spend eternity."

"I doubt it," she says.

"Doubt this is heaven, doubt that I died, doubt that you spend eternity anywhere?"

I see confusion in her expression and let the matter drop. Finally I say, "So?"

"So?" she responds.

Not able to contain myself any longer I say, "You have to tell me. The suspense is killing me."

"Alright," she agrees. "You want to know why I asked you out for dinner? Is that right?"

"No, actually I was wondering where we spend eternity, but that was my second question."

She smiles. "Partly because of your eyes."

"My eyes? You're spending an evening with me because of my eyes? They're behind glasses. You can't even see them."

"I can see them."

"And the other part?" I ask.

"I like people and I'm interested in their lives. Besides, it seemed like a nice thing to do since you were alone."

Just then the waitress arrives to take our order. "One check?" she asks.

"Yeah. She's paying," I say flippantly.

I'm startled by my own comment. Where do my thoughts come from?

Embarrassed I add, "Just kidding, I'm paying." The waitress takes our order and leaves.

"First ground rule," Jean informs me, "we pay our own way."

"Okay," I agree, "but how many rules are there? I didn't bring a notebook and I have a selective memory."

"We'll make them up as we go."

I decide to use the restroom and nervously glance around to see where it is. I don't see any signs so I ask Jean if she knows where it is.

"Around the corner and down the short hallway," she says.

My first response is to ask her to write this down, but instead I thank her and excuse myself. I concentrate on remembering where the table is in relation to the restroom. This is no time to get confused. I exit the restroom and, sure enough, I'm lost. Our waitress spots my confusion and directs me back to my table. Hesitantly, I sit down and wait for Jean to tease. She doesn't.

We eat dinner slowly as I answer her questions. I tell her about my family, my ex-wife Sheila, my daughter Emily, and my son Mark. I describe my former businesses. I tell her life doesn't make sense, that for me, it's like trying to fill round holes with square pegs. I smile at the analogy and wonder where that came from too. I ramble on about questioning the universe, finding meaning in life and searching for enlightenment. I even explain a little how New Jersey is on the way to California.

Jean listens intently and seems interested.

Then she tells me about herself. She has a master's

degree in counseling, worked as a therapist, and even had a small private practice for a few years. She was married, but divorced about eight years ago. Jean avoids a lot of details. Since then she's dated a little, but there hasn't been anything serious. For the last five years she's been a real estate agent, thanks to Stuart Crawley. She enjoys being near the ocean and takes walks on the beach before work every morning and whenever she can at night.

Eventually the waitress clears the table and knows we plan to stay and enjoy the moonlight on the bay. If the evening stopped right now, it might be my all-time favorite. I'll decide that later after I have more time to think about it.

We sit quietly for a few minutes. Finally Jean says, "This has been a pleasant evening, Alan."

The comment surprises me. "That's good. I thought I drove people crazy. In fact, I'm discovering that I drive myself crazy. I can't escape my own thoughts. They just keep coming."

"Tell me more," she encourages.

We spend what seems like several days as I recount details of my life and thoughts. I pause, look at Jean and ask, "Is that what you see in my eyes?"

"Some of it," she admits. "I see two different people. Outwardly, you're one person, but your eyes express something different."

I smile and note a lump in my throat.

For a long time we sit and look at the water. My body seems to be at rest, but my thoughts are going full speed.

"You *do* think a lot, don't you?" she says.

"How can you tell?"

"I can feel them. Thoughts are energy and have tremendous power."

"I've read that," I admit, "but I don't understand how that's possible."

"Maybe we can discuss it some time."

That's promising, I think. She wants to be with me again. "Maybe," I say to her.

After a period of silence, I turn to Jean and ask, "What are you thinking?"

"I'm not thinking," she answers. "I'm feeling."

I think to myself, I don't understand that. I'm not sure what feeling is. To me, all outside phenomena are funneled to my brain where they get categorized. Based on that, I react automatically from fear and anxiety. I remember Sheila asking me one time if I was having fun riding my bike on the boardwalk. I answered, "I think so, but I'll know better tomorrow after the experience sinks in."

When people talk about living in the moment, I have no idea what they mean. My thoughts are concerned with the past and the future. I'm either worrying about something that has happened or anxious about something that will happen. The present gets lost.

Jean is perceptive and notices my distraction. "I can tell you're definitely a 'thinking' person. Maybe you were hoping to find 'feelings' in California."

I make a strange face hoping she'll laugh. "If feelings are a part of enlightenment, then I suppose I was searching for them too."

She touches me on the arm as she smiles.

We enjoy each other's company and a memorable evening passes. The waitress walks back and informs us they're ready to close. Jean allows me to leave the tip but reminds me that we pay for our own dinners. As we walk towards the car I say, "This evening has been wonderful."

"Yes it has," she agrees. "I've really enjoyed it."

Motorcycle Enlightenment

We drive to the apartment and stop outside. "I need to go," Jean says. "I have a busy day tomorrow."

I take a gulp of air to ask . . .

"Yes," she answers, "I'd like to see you again." Then, a delightful smile, a little wave and she's gone.

I stand on the sidewalk wondering if this whole evening has been a dream. I'll replay it many times in my thoughts.

5.

I'm sleeping in this morning because not having anything to do makes me tired. I lie in bed and think about Jean. I picture her shoulder-length brown hair pulled back and fastened with a clip. I see her delightful smile and blue eyes. I could disappear in those eyes. They're soft and reach out as if to say, "It's okay. Everything will be okay." I felt better being around her, like life has a purpose after all. You know how some people make you feel at ease the moment they walk into a room. That's Jean.

My thoughts float here and there and I follow them. Come to think of it, I've always done that. I remember times when life seemed to be going smoothly, and, suddenly, from out of nowhere, a thought rushed in and made me sad. I wouldn't know where it came from, but I'd become depressed by an avalanche of thoughts. And that mood would last until another thought sent me in another direction.

This morning, fortunately, random good thoughts appear. In fact, the thought of doughnuts pops into my mind and eating seems like a good idea. I get up, shower and dress. As I'm putting on my shirt I think: I'm all dressed up with no place to work. I didn't think I would miss work this much. I always hated it, but now that I'm not working, freedom's not so great either. All my life I dreamed of the day I wouldn't have to work. Now it's here and I'm lost.

I start to open the front door and see Mrs. Crawley working in the yard. My reaction is to go out the backdoor so I don't have to say hello. My second thought is the same, so I go out the backdoor. I walk at least four blocks out of my way to avoid saying good morning. There's something wrong with that.

It's only ten A.M. and bike riding is permitted until eleven. I walk to the 13th Street bike rental again and look for the same bike. I fall into habits easily. I rationalize the bike decision by telling myself that the bike I rented yesterday rode smoothly, so why should I take a chance on another one. This line of reasoning makes sense, and I find the same bike with the same streak of red paint on the chain guard. The attendant sees me and smiles. This leads me to wonder whether he's being friendly or laughing at me because I asked him to write down the directions to the telephone office.

"Hi, nice to see you again," he says. "Pleasant morning for a ride."

I quickly replay the comments in my mind and categorize them as friendly and respond, "Yes, it is."

I pay for the bike and start up the ramp, postviewing the conversation two or three times. I decide it was a passable encounter because I handled the situation well. So I can go back there again and feel at ease.

I handle every conversation, in fact every situation, past or future, in this manner. I preview every conversation in advance. As it's taking place, I'm in a panic and feel nervous, missing the actual moment itself. Later I postview the conversation endlessly to see how it went.

This is exhausting. I convince myself that I actually saved energy by not speaking to Mrs. Crawley this morning.

I pedal the bike in slow motion as close to the ocean side of the boardwalk as allowed. I stare at the ocean half the time and at people the other half. Many look familiar because I saw them riding bicycles or jogging yesterday. I observe faces and eyes carefully to see if people are happy or sad.

Today I ride to the doughnut shop and buy three doughnuts with the same color sprinkles as yesterday. I ride to the far end of the boardwalk, sit at the same place on the same bench, look at the same Atlantic City, eat my doughnuts and ride back. I turn in the bike at 11:05. Now what do I do?

I walk back up the ramp to the boardwalk and slowly stroll toward the real estate office. I know I can't bother Jean at work, and I know I'm headed there only because I don't have anything else to do. I walk to a section of the boardwalk where there are benches under a roof. Most of the seats are taken, but I find an empty one facing the ocean and sit down.

I stay so long that I outlast all the other sitters. By one a new crowd appears. Where was I all morning? Lost in thought?

It's lunch time so I head for the pizza shop. On the way I remember the microwave and frozen food and consider whether I should eat at the apartment and save money. After a few minutes of deliberation I decide the frozen food will keep and that I deserve pizza today. I walk along trying to figure out why I deserve pizza since I haven't done anything but eat and sleep for two days. And there doesn't appear to be any immediate change in my near future.

Motorcycle Enlightenment

I eat two slices of pizza and drink a Pepsi. I ponder whether I should sit here in Angelo's for three more hours so I can order more pizza for dinner. Fortunately, I have another thought and decide to walk on the beach.

I leave Angelo's, walk down the steps to the beach and take off my shoes and socks. I love the shore and the ocean, but I'm not fond of sitting on the beach. No matter where I put my blanket, the person next to me will play music too loud. There might be one other person on the beach for twenty miles, and he'll sit beside me and turn on a radio. That, and playing paddle ball. Why do they always play paddle ball in front of me? They use my beach chair as their out-of-bounds marker. That, and throwing Frisbees. I'm a magnet for these things. The beach can be deserted until I show up. Within two minutes someone will come, put down a blanket and turn on music. While I get irritated I'll get hit in the front by a paddle ball and in the back with a Frisbee.

I stuff my socks into my tennis shoes and tie the shoes to my belt loops. It looks funny but I don't care. Along the water's edge the sand is cool and the water cold. If I walked along the ocean like this for several years, I wonder if I'd run out of thoughts.

The sand and water are a balm, releasing my troubles with every breath. My shoulders, normally up around my ears, relax a few inches. I walk without focusing on anything until a beautiful girl runs by. She catches my attention and I stare, at least until I see a male twice my size chasing her into the water. My thoughts go back to neutral.

Eventually I stop walking and gaze around to get my bearings. I have none. But at least I know I'm not lost because the water's still on my left. Looking back from the direction I came, I see it was impossible to have walked on the beach the whole way because the water is under the boardwalk and deep at some places. Unconsciously, I must have walked up the steps, along the boardwalk and back down to the beach.

This doesn't surprise me. When I was a teacher, I used to drive home from school without knowing it. I would pull the car into the driveway and wonder how I got there because the route went through a small town with four traffic lights. Since I wouldn't remember driving through the town or seeing the lights, I had no idea whether I had stopped or driven through them. Sometimes I would sit in the car and wait a few minutes to see if police cars showed up. When none did, I knew I hadn't run over anybody.

I walk so far that I'm tired and don't know if I have the energy to return. A small sand dune looks like an ideal place to rest. I sit down, take a few deep breaths, and I'm out. I sleep sitting up, a skill I developed in college.

Later when I awaken, I don't know where I am. But, putting my hand down refreshes my memory. I'm sitting in the sand without a blanket. Thoughts flow rapidly and I can't stop them. I'll have to wash my clothes. I don't want to think about that now. Too late. They continue. Where's the laundromat? Will I know how to work the washer and dryer? How do I put in the detergent? Suppose someone used dye in the washer and my underwear comes out pink? Suppose my pants and shirts come out wrinkled? I can't iron. All this from touching sand.

I brush the sand off my pants and shirt. It's 5:45 P.M. and I'm a long way from the apartment, and not certain whether Ocean City has taxi service. I decide that walking back on the sand will be tiring, so I head for the

Motorcycle Enlightenment

street. Sitting on the curb I brush the sand off my feet. To get it out from between my toes I use my socks. Then I have to brush off my socks. I'm having doubts about whether this was a good idea.

6.

A car horn beeps and scares me, making me wonder if it's illegal to clean my feet on the curb. Looking up I see Jean pulling her car off to the side of the road. She gets out and walks over.

"What in the world are you doing?"

"Brushing sand off my feet," I say with some trepidation.

She laughs.

"Seriously. What are you doing?"

"Well, truthfully, I walked too far, sat down on the sand, without a blanket I might add, fell asleep and was just now wondering how I would get home."

"You poor man," she says as she sits down, puts her arm around me and pulls me close.

I put my head on her shoulder. "Can we stay like this the rest of our lives?"

"Like this?" she wonders.

"Exactly like this."

"Won't you get hungry or cold?"

"No."

"No?" she says, amused. "Are you sure you won't get cold?"

I sit up and look at her. "What do you know about

cold weather and me?" How could she know I'm always cold?

She reaches over and tugs my shirt sleeve. "How many people were on the beach in long sleeve shirts today?"

"I don't know. I didn't see anyone else," I reply honestly.

Now she's perplexed. "There were thousands of people on the beach," she informs me.

Remembering the attractive girl and her partner I make a correction. "I saw two people," I say, somewhat proud of my observation.

She looks at me but I feel as if she's looking into me.

"So," she summarizes, "You saw two people and you were cold."

"Right," I agree. "Most of the time I was lost in thought, I suppose, and it was very cold this morning when I started out."

"It was 70 degrees," she says emphatically.

"See," I say, proving my point.

She brushes the sand off my feet while I stare incredulously. She stops and asks, "Why are you staring?"

"Because you're cleaning my feet."

"I know. What's wrong with that?"

"Nothing." But I think to myself, this is very different. Someone is being kind and gentle to me and, quite honestly, that hasn't happened for awhile. I've forgotten how it feels. But I think it's good.

We get into her car and drive back to my apartment.

"Would you like to come in," I ask, "or are you busy tonight?"

"I can come in."

My eyes light up. "Really?"

"Really," she says with a different inflection.

Uh oh, I think to myself. My bachelor friend told me about the sequence. First a pleasant evening together, then the careful letdown. I feel myself becoming defensive.

"You're a nice person," she says.

"And . . . ?" I quickly add.

"And you're a nice person," she repeats, stopping to contemplate the tone in my voice.

We walk inside and select chairs on opposite sides of the room. She looks at me and says, "Something's not quite right. I don't believe there are any coincidences about meeting people at certain times in our lives. As soon as you walked into the real estate office I liked you. Last night was enjoyable and I felt comfortable. I'd like to see where this goes, but I'm not in a hurry."

"Is this about me?" I question.

"No, it's just the way it is," she responds. "I like ground rules because they help prevent expectations. I'd like to spend some time with you. Maybe something will work out and maybe it won't."

I open my mouth.

"I don't know more than that right now."

I close my mouth.

"Let's just watch and be patient. If that's asking too much, I understand."

"No, it's okay," I say too nonchalantly.

"I mean it," she says seriously.

Somehow I think she means it very seriously.

"Sure," I say this time and mean it.

Jean takes a deep breath, and I can tell she feels a major obstacle has been lifted.

I wait awhile and ask, "Are you hungry?"

"A little," she says. "What did you eat today?"

"Doughnuts and pizza," I answer.

"That's it? Doughnuts and pizza?"

"Well, the doughnuts had sprinkles on them, and I had a Pepsi with my pizza."

Not being familiar with her I can't decipher her expression.

I get an idea. "We can eat here tonight if you'd like."

"Sure, that would be nice."

We walk to the refrigerator and she opens the door. "There's nothing here!"

"It's in the freezer," I reply matter-of-factly.

Opening it she sees the frozen entrees plus ice cream and Cool Whip. "That's all you have?"

I nod.

"So," Jean concludes, "for a home-cooked meal you put a frozen package into the microwave and nuke it?"

I consider the phrasing to see if I can make it more palatable. Unable to, I agree, "Yeah, that's basically it."

"Oh, boy," she sighs, "have we got work to do."

Somehow I know the work she's referring to isn't the kind I either like or want to do.

"Let's go out tonight," Jean relents.

"I like the sound of that," I tell her. "Maybe I'll find a job so I can eat out every night."

"I think you should learn how to cook," she suggests.

Maybe she's right but I'm not anxious to find out.

A few minutes later we're sitting at the Peking Restaurant waiting for an order of mixed vegetables, white rice and tofu.

"Are you sure this goes with doughnuts and pizza?" I ask.

At first Jean dismisses the comment but reconsiders.

"Vegetables are necessary. Your body needs them."

"I know they are," I agree. "It's just so much work to cook them."

I can't read this expression either. Maybe it's incredulousness.

Our waiter brings huge portions of rice, vegetables and chunks of something white. I can only identify three of the vegetables Jean puts on her plate. I dish out the rice and neatly pile it on mine. Next I pick through the vegetables and take out the broccoli, snow peas and baby ears of corn and place them beside the rice. I look carefully at the white, rubbery stuff but don't take any.

"You don't like tofu?" Jean asks.

"No."

"Have you ever tried it?"

"No," I answer defensively.

"Do you decide whether you like food by looking at it rather than tasting it?"

"Maybe," I grumble.

"It all gets mixed together in your stomach anyway," she jokes.

"I don't like to think about what food does in my stomach."

If I let myself admit it, the meal was delicious. We pay our bill and stroll to the car. After driving back to the apartment we go inside. Jean sits down in the chair on the far side of the room and I half-recline on the couch.

"I haven't eaten so much food in days, maybe weeks," I tell her.

"Within a month you could be cooking like that."

"Me? Are you sure?"

"I have no doubt," she says.

I'm not sure I believe her.

Motorcycle Enlightenment

"Would you like to watch television or listen to music?" I ask. She can tell I'm nervous.

"Relax," she says, "pretend I'm your sister and just be normal."

"I never had a sister and I'm not certain what normal is anymore. I've been disoriented for some time."

She smiles and my tension eases.

"Why don't you play some music and we'll sit quietly and relax?"

I put on a tape of soothing piano music. After a few minutes Jean closes her eyes and leans back in the chair. I sit and watch the glare of the setting sun on the apartment building across the street.

Jean opens her eyes. "On the outside you appear to be very calm, but inside your thoughts apparently drive you crazy." She stands up and walks over to the couch, sits down and motions for me to put my head on her lap.

I take off my shoes and lie down. I'm in heaven, I remind myself, so don't miss it.

As I lie there, she gently strokes my forehead. "Lie still and breathe," she says. "Follow your breath into your abdomen, and whenever your thoughts wander, bring them back with your breath."

I feel the tension begin to release from my body. My thoughts are on my breath, occasionally.

"Better," she says as if she can feel my thoughts.

I raise up to ask a question.

"I can feel you relax," she says, answering the question I didn't ask.

She continues stroking my forehead and I rest peacefully.

The click of the music tape ending startles me, and I realize I fell asleep.

"You slept for about a half-hour," she says.

I immediately sit up and express guilt that she pampered me.

"It's okay," she says. "While you were sleeping, two images came to me. One was a huge spider making a web. Suddenly a big 'X' was drawn over it."

"Gosh. What's that about?"

"Maybe a sign of caution," she states. "I'll see what comes to me later. The second one," she continues, "was a large wheel with a hub in the middle and spokes reaching outward. This was superimposed over the world and I saw you at the hub. The spokes became veins or routes across the world."

"What could that mean? Maybe it has something to do with finding meaning in my life. I've always been looking for that niche where I fit."

Jean redirects me. "You seem to think that you don't fit in anywhere. You do. Just relax and live in the moment."

"Where's that?"

She begins to stand up. "I have to go. Tomorrow is a work day."

"Not for everyone," I add.

"But you said you're not happy when you're not working," she reminds me.

"I know. I have too much time to spend with myself."

We walk to the car.

"Will I see you soon?" I ask.

"I'm not sure. I'll have to see how the week goes."

I wave as she drives away. Walking into the house I get the feeling my life is going to change and I might not have the chance to preview it. Suppose I just have to live it? I start to worry.

7.

A constant, light tapping on the door awakens me. After adjusting to my surroundings, I realize someone is knocking on the front door. Jumping out of bed, I grab my robe, head downstairs and open the door to see a radiant-looking Jean.

"Good morning," she says.

"Morning doesn't start till nine," I reply. "What are you doing here? But, more important, what time is it?"

"It's six A.M., Sunday, and it's a beautiful day," she responds with such enthusiasm I'm almost tempted to believe her. "Would you like to go walking on the beach?"

"Now?" I ask. I ponder it for a minute. The offer does sound inviting. "It would take me awhile to get ready unless I can go in my pajamas and robe."

"Not really," she answers, "Can you be ready in fifteen minutes? And, while you're getting ready, I'll prepare you a quick breakfast."

I turn and sprint up the steps two at a time. I run into the bathroom, brush my teeth and wash my face. I think, this might be the only time I've ever been glad that I was bald. There's no such thing as a bad hair day.

I hear a voice at the bottom of the stairs. "Alan, you

don't have anything to eat for breakfast. Not even bread for toast."

"I know. I was going to get something one of these days."

"What were you planning to have for breakfast today?"

Suddenly that's a difficult question. If I say doughnuts, she'd probably think it's a bad idea. If I say nothing until I had pizza for lunch, she'd probably think that's worse. "I hadn't thought that far ahead," I reply. "Maybe I would have gone out for breakfast."

No response. I suppose that answer was sufficient.

I'm down the steps in twelve minutes.

"Good timing," Jean says, "but I wish you had something to eat before you walk on the beach."

"We'll walk for awhile and have breakfast on the boardwalk," I suggest.

We walk up the ramp to the boardwalk, across and down the other side.

"I'm so glad you decided to walk with me this morning," she says.

"My pleasure," I tell her, and mumble under my breath, "Even if it is too early."

There's a sense of excitement as we walk. Eventually we stop and look at the path of sunlight stretching across the ocean. I feel as if I could follow it to the sun. A few seagulls are standing motionless on the sand. In front of us little shore birds, the ones that run toward the boardwalk when a wave breaks and toward the ocean when the water recedes, are running back and forth without getting wet.

"What are you thinking?" I ask Jean.

"I'm not thinking. I'm feeling," she replies.

"What are you feeling?" I try again. "I'm feeling relaxed and just enjoying the moment. And you?" she asks.

"I think," I pause, "I think I feel pretty good."

She looks at me and says, "Don't take this the wrong way, but. . ."

My "pretty good" is sinking fast.

"Maybe you spend so much time thinking you've turned off feeling."

I look at her and nod. "Jean," I say honestly, "I'm sure that's true."

We both take large, long sighs. "Well," she says, "I think it's time for breakfast."

"Where?" I ask. To me, we're as lost as if we were marooned on a desert island. It's been a long time since I saw the last recognizable landmark, although I probably could find my way back: water to the right, land to the left.

Walking toward the houses I ask Jean, "Would you like to own one of these?"

"Not really," she replies. "Would you?"

"Sure, like that one." I point to a two-story house with a glass-enclosed patio on the first level and a screened-in porch on the second.

"Why?" she asks.

I pause to consider. "Well, because it would make me happy."

We walk to a small restaurant and sit at a booth. I have an image of Jean sitting here with someone else. My thoughts quickly pull me towards a feeling of sadness, but I try to push them away. Too late.

She reaches across the table and taps my hand. My guilty eyes look up. "How do you know when I'm thinking too much?" I ask.

"Remember the saying that people wear their hearts on their sleeves? Well, you display your mind through your breath. You have distinct breathing patterns. When you get lost in thought, your breath is short and shallow. When you're at ease, your breath is long and deep. And, besides, your eyes tell everything about you."

"So if I want to keep any secrets, I need to wear sunglasses and stop breathing?"

"The first might work for awhile. The other for about a minute," Jean replies.

After we finish eating she looks at me and asks candidly, "Why do I keep getting this impression that there are two Alans?"

"I guess I'm schizophrenic."

"I'm serious. The thinking you always seems tense and worried, but the relaxed you is very different."

"I guess I keep the relaxed me hidden and only let him out when it's safe."

"And when is it safe?" she wonders.

"I wish I knew."

We leave the restaurant and head for the beach.

"I know you're right," I say.

"About?"

"About there being two Alans."

"I think so," she agrees.

"One part of me is afraid and withdraws quickly while another part feels as if it's peering out at the world and wants to emerge, as if from a cocoon."

"I know the feeling," Jean says.

I look at her eyes, brush her hair behind her ear, and start to ask about her comment. She places her finger on my lips, silently asking me not to question her.

I gently remove her finger but hold her hand. We sort

of embrace, awkwardly. She steps back and begins walking. I sigh and follow.

She finds a sand dune and sits down. I brush some shells away, smooth the sand, and join her. I get comfortable and close my eyes. For some reason there are no thoughts and I disappear into my breath. Time elapses, and when I open my eyes I see Jean standing at the water's edge. I approach quietly, wrap my arms around her, and pretend to throw her into the water. She lets out a scream and laughs.

"You scared me. I thought you were going to throw me in," she gasps with shock and delight.

"I would never do that," I assure her.

For a moment time stops. We hug. This time a little less awkwardly and with a little more emotion. But it's shortlived.

"Let's walk farther," she says. "And while we're walking, tell me more about yourself."

"If you tell me some things too," I bargain.

She doesn't answer.

"What would you like to know?" I ask.

"About life in general."

"That's how my son and I used to start our conversations. I'd look at him and ask, 'So, what do you think?' He'd say, 'About what?' I'd answer, 'Life in general.' Unfortunately we often didn't go much further. . . . Life in general. That's a hard question. Let's see. I guess for starters I don't know why I'm here. It's like there's been a time warp and I ended up in the wrong world. Like I told you, I never seem to fit in. I've spent my life searching for answers to the questions, Who am I, Why am I here, and What is the purpose of life?" I stop and look at Jean and add my new question, "And why does Jean want to spend time with me?"

She seemingly ignores the last question. "So, let me get this straight. You basically spend all your time trying to figure out the meaning of life."

"Yes."

"And where has that gotten you?"

"Right here."

She looks at me, doesn't say a word, and continues sauntering along the water's edge.

"Well, then, what do you like to do?"

"Usually, anything but what I am doing."

She looks confused so I try to clarify it. "No matter what I'm doing, I always have the feeling that I would rather be doing something else, like another choice would have been better."

After a few minutes she sighs and says, "With that frame of mind, how do you get through each day?"

"With difficulty," I answer half-jokingly. "I guess I just developed my own coping mechanism."

We walk a distance farther. I stop again and look into Jean's eyes. "I never told anyone this before, but some nights I would drive home after work, go to bed and wish I wouldn't get up in the morning. Other nights I would lie on the bed, look at the ceiling and implore, 'Here's a human body. What do you want to do with it?'"

"Who were you asking?"

"I don't know. I just thought there had to be someone or something higher or greater than me that knew what was going on. There had to be something more to life than what I experienced on the surface."

"Did you get any answers?"

"I guess not. Here I am. If this is the answer, I don't understand it. So, I'll keep searching. But you can answer one of my questions."

"I don't think so."

"Sure you can. Why are you spending time with me?"

"Why are you surprised that a woman would enjoy your company?"

Everything stops for a moment. This is a new thought. "Well, Jean," I consider, "I've never been with anyone but Sheila. We met as teenagers. And I know she didn't enjoy being with me, especially during the last years of our marriage when I was depressed and unhappy. And, honestly, I don't like being with me either. So . . . ."

"I see, Alan." Somehow my explanation changes something. She breathes deeply. "I too had a difficult period in my life not long ago. I was involved in a very unhappy marriage. My husband Edward was jealous and even suspicious of my clients. Then when I started attending meditation classes, he became increasingly angry. He said he wasn't interested in 'spiritual stuff' and he didn't think I should be either. Things kept getting worse until I simply couldn't stay any longer. And yet, when I left, I was devastated. Stuart and Alice Crawley helped me put the pieces back together.

"When you walked into my office, I had a good feeling about you. And then when you told me about your search for enlightenment and your quest for the meaning of life, I was intrigued. So, to answer your question, I guess I want to find out more about you. But . . ." She stops.

"But?" I repeat.

"I know I still have lots of work to do on myself," she confesses.

"I wouldn't have guessed. Your life looks perfect to me."

We continue walking in silence. Jean steers me across the sand and back towards the street. Again I forget she knows where she is. We walk a few blocks and stop.

"Your house?" I ask.

"Yes."

"Very attractive."

We walk inside and I immediately feel at home.

"Sit down," she suggests. "I'll get you something to drink."

When she returns I've melted into a chair, a swivel-rocker.

"My, you look comfortable," Jean says.

"I do feel comfortable. I could live here."

"No offense, but you're not invited," she quickly adds.

"No offense taken," I assure her.

She turns on a tape of solo flute music and sits down on the floor in front of me. Tentatively I rub her neck and shoulders and she doesn't seem to mind.

At this moment I'm as close to the present as I've ever been.

8.

It's Monday morning and the telephone company is connecting my service at ten. I sleep late, don't have enough time to go out for breakfast, and don't have anything to eat at home. I open the freezer and consider having a beef pie but change my mind. Later today, I tell myself, I'm getting some frozen breakfasts.

At 9:58 a service technician knocks on the door, and fifteen minutes later she's finished with the installation. But, when she asks for my phone to see if it works, I realize I have no phone.

I think there must be some communication symbolism in that.

On the way downtown to purchase a telephone I pass a bakery and buy a muffin. Jean would be proud of me—it doesn't have sugar sprinkles on top. I head for a store, find the electronics department, pick up a cordless phone, carry it to the counter and purchase it.

Comedians joke about the "shopping gene." I don't have one. I don't like shopping. The idea of looking at three or four models of the same item in order to decide which is best pushes me to the brink of insanity. Clever advertisers have their way with me. For instance, I have no idea why I purchased the phone I did. Maybe the box was taller, wider, or redder. Anyway you look at it, I have a phone and I'm on my way home to plug it in.

Reading directions is another one of my aversions. Somehow this is coupled with the fact that I have no mechanical skills. So whether I buy a cordless phone or computer program, I figure the manufacturer knows a small percentage of the population can't read or understand the directions and most everyone else doesn't bother to look at them. So products have to be easy to operate.

At home I unpack the box, take parts out of the plastic bags, plug them together and presto, it looks like a phone. I pick up the receiver to see if it works. Nothing. Why doesn't it work? "Ah," I say, "I bet it runs on a battery and needs to charge." I place the receiver on the base, see a red light that indicates the battery is charging, and go about my business.

Only problem is I have no business. It's Monday morning, 11:30, and I have nothing to do for the whole week. I sit down and stare out the window. Soon I'm reclining on the couch. Soon I'm sound asleep. I wake up at 1:30.

Today I decide to make my own lunch. I select a beef pie, put it in the microwave and sit down to eat fifteen minutes later. I can barely choke it down. I make a mental note to ask Jean if she's serious about giving me cooking lessons.

Suddenly I have an inspired thought. I decide to surprise Jean by purchasing a steamer. Although I have no idea how it works, I saw an advertisement on television that said a steamer is ideal for cooking rice and vegetables. Jean likes to eat rice and vegetables. That's a match to me.

I walk back to the same store where I purchased the

telephone. The clerk looks surprised and thinks I'm back to return the phone, but when she sees me empty handed she greets me, "Hello, back already?"

"Yes," I say. "I'm looking for a steamer."

"What kind?" she asks.

"One that steams rice and vegetables."

She pauses, waiting to hear if more information is forthcoming. There is none so she informs me, "They all do that."

"Great. Would you pick one out for me?"

She walks over to the kitchen appliance aisle and takes one off the shelf. "I have this one and I really like it."

"I do too," I say.

"I wish all my customers were as easy to please as you."

"I don't have the shopping gene," I tell her. I leave the store postviewing the conversation and decide it went well.

As I walk towards the front door of my apartment, Mrs. Crawley opens her door to come out.

"Good afternoon, Alan."

"Hello, Mrs. Crawley, how are you?"

"Fine," she answers and adds, "Are you enjoying the apartment?"

"Yes I am. Thank you for renting it to me. It feels like home."

"You're a good tenant, Alan. Sometimes people aren't the way they describe themselves when they want to rent it. But you said you were quiet and you really are. I haven't heard a sound from your side of the house."

"And you won't," I assure her, "unless Jean visits and makes too much noise."

She laughs. "I doubt that will happen. I'm glad you

two are getting along. I like to hear her laugh, and I've heard her laughing with you."

"At me," I correct, "but I guess that still counts."

She pats me on the back and says, "I like you." Unable to resist looking at the package in my arms she asks, "What did you buy?"

"A steamer," I say.

"Oh, so you cook?"

"Not really. I can use a microwave and that's it. But Jean told me she's going to give me some basic cooking instructions, so I thought I should get ready. Honestly I don't know how this thing works."

She looks at me and thinks I'm kidding. My facial expression tells the truth. "Oh, you're serious," she says. "Well, it steams vegetables. It's simple."

"Really?" I say surprised.

"Really." I see a quick change in her expression. "I've got an idea. Why don't you call Jean and invite her over for dinner? I'll help you get everything prepared and you can surprise her."

"Shock may be more the word, but it sounds like fun."

"Let's call Jean at work."

Mrs. Crawley opens her door and shows me to the phone. She stands beside me as I dial.

"Hello. Ocean City Real Estate. Jean speaking. May I help you?"

"Hello, Jean. This is Alan. Do you have a minute? I want to ask you a quick question."

"Sure," she says.

"Would you be interested in coming over for dinner this evening? I'm cooking."

There's a long pause. "You're cooking? Does that mean I have my choice of a chicken or beef pie?"

Motorcycle Enlightenment

"No, I can tell you that it will be edible, but I can't tell you what it is."

Mrs. Crawley stands behind me laughing. She knows I can't tell Jean what it is because I have no idea myself.

"What time?" Jean asks.

"What time," I repeat loud enough so Mrs. Crawley hears.

"Six-thirty," she whispers to me.

I repeat "six-thirty" to Jean.

"Is someone there with you?" Jean asks.

"Why do you ask?"

"No reason, see you then. I'll be looking forward to this."

"So will I. I mean, good, me too."

Mrs. Crawley and I walk to the grocery store. On the way we talk about Ocean City and how it's changed. I tell her that I've been coming here for about twenty-five years. She tells me she's lived here for over fifty years.

"You know," she says, "I just turned sixty-five this spring."

"No. I would never have guessed that. I thought you were probably in your late fifties, not a lot older than I am."

"That was a perfect compliment," she teases.

"I'm serious," I insist. "You always look so happy. Maybe that's what makes you look younger."

"I attribute my life philosophy to my late husband Stuart. He was a wonderful man."

"Jean's mentioned him. I'd like to know more about him."

She nods in agreement with my comment just as we arrive at the store.

Mrs. Crawley selects Basmati rice, broccoli, snow peas and tofu. "We won't make this too difficult or Jean will never believe you did it yourself."

"Did it myself?" I say surprised. "I thought you were doing it."

"I'm helping," she corrects. "I'm not doing it for you."

Back at the apartment Mrs. Crawley writes down easy directions for me to follow. She instructs me to fill the bottom portion of the steamer to the "high fill" line, to measure rice and water and put them in the rice basket, and to cut the broccoli and de-string the snow peas. She marinates the tofu in a sauce which she brings from her house.

"Jean will never believe I prepared this."

"Yes, she will," Mrs. Crawley assures me, "and she'll commend your effort."

We have everything ready to go by 5:30. The rice is on and the vegetables are ready. The tofu is in the oven.

"You're on your own from here. When the timer goes off, carefully remove the rice basket, place it on this trivet and cover it with this bowl. Take the basket out and put the vegetables in. Then put this in"—she holds up what I called the juice catcher—"put the big basket on top and set the timer for another ten minutes. Can you do that?"

"I hope so."

"That's all there is to it. Just be careful because burns are very painful. Keep your face and hands away from the steam," she warns me.

"Thank you, Mrs. Crawley. I really appreciate your help. This was one of the best days I've had in Ocean City."

Motorcycle Enlightenment

She pats me on the back. "Hope everything goes okay. See you later."

The timer goes off and I go into action. I follow all the directions but forget the juice catcher. My first thought is to skip it, but my second thought is I better use it. I carefully take off the vegetable basket, but put my right thumb in the steam. I drop the tray, jump back and knock the vegetables on the floor. Quickly I turn on the faucet and run cold water on my thumb. It's painful.

I glance at the clock—6:15. I look at the floor—vegetables everywhere.

Despite the pain I pick up the vegetables with my hands, put them into the basket and restart the steamer. I grab a paper towel, which Mrs. Crawley thoughtfully bought, and begin cleaning up. I wonder if I should have rinsed off the vegetables after they were on the floor. Too late. They're steaming now.

At 6:27 the timer goes off. I hope Jean's on time because I have no idea how to warm this up if it gets cold, unless it goes in the microwave.

At 6:33 Jean knocks on the door.

"Come in," I say, "dinner's ready."

"I don't believe this. Is it catered?"

"No, I did it myself," I assure her and hold up my red thumb for proof.

"You're serious," she says.

"We better sit down and eat before it gets cold," I suggest as I start filling the plates.

Jean takes a bite of the vegetables first. "This is good." She tastes the tofu and says loudly enough for someone listening at the wall, "I love your sauce, Alice. Thank you."

I knew marinating the tofu would give it away.

After dinner Jean helps with clean up, washing the dishes and putting them away.

"Do you know what I would enjoy doing this evening?" she asks.

"No idea," I respond.

"Watching a movie."

"I have a few of my favorites with me."

"Great. What are they?"

I go upstairs, pull them out of the closet and bring them down. She looks over the selection and decides on my favorite comedy, *Annie Hall*. For the rest of the evening we're sitting on the couch, watching the movie and laughing.

After it's over Jean says, "You know, when you relax you breathe so evenly and deeply. If you were more aware of your breath, you would know when you begin to think too much."

"I'm afraid if I concentrate on my breath, it might stop."

She looks at me with a skeptical expression.

Finally Jean says, "I really must go. I have to be at work early in the morning. What are you doing tomorrow?"

"I've been thinking about buying a computer. Maybe tomorrow's the day."

"Really?" she says with enthusiasm. "Why?"

"So I can write a book."

"What about?"

"A man who is totally lost but manages to become enlightened as he rides his motorcycle across the United States."

"Is this autobiographical?"

"Semi."

Motorcycle Enlightenment

"So you're riding your motorcycle to California?"

I take a moment to reflect on bodily pain. "No. Maybe my character will find enlightenment as he flies from city to city across the United States."

"First class?" she asks.

"Of course." I'm beginning to like this idea more already.

9.

I wake up startled. I look at the clock and see that it's two A.M. I have this feeling that someone was talking to me, but I don't know who it was or what they said. I do know that my breath is short and shallow so I lie back and breathe deeply. As clear as can be I hear the voice again. It says, "You have been told that out of the darkness came light, but I tell you now that out of the light came darkness and out of the darkness comes light."

I look around the room to see who's speaking, but no one is here. I get out of bed, feel my way to the light and turn it on. I take my notebook and pen, which are lying on the bureau, and write down what I heard.

I want to go downstairs and call Jean but decide against it. I want to go back to sleep but I'm reluctant to lie down. So I stand in the room and think about the voice. Actually, it was reassuring, if not comforting. Eventually I lie down again and fall into a restful sleep.

In the morning I remember the incident as clearly as if it were happening again. I get out of bed, walk to the bureau and look at the sentence written in the notebook. It's sloppily written but readable. It wasn't a dream.

I go downstairs and call Jean at work. Another realtor answers and I have to hold a few minutes. During this time I have second thoughts about telling her what happened over the phone. But before I can hang up she answers.

"Hello, Alan?"

"Jean, I had the strangest experience last night."

"What happened?"

I begin telling her the details of what I remember.

"Alan," Jean interrupts, "I'd like to hear more about this, but, unfortunately, I'm really busy at the moment."

Instantly I'm disappointed.

"Alan," she says, "are you there?"

"Yeah."

"I would like to hear about it but I'm at work, and busy. We'll have to talk later, okay?"

"Okay. See you sometime. Goodbye."

Suddenly I'm in a bad mood. I sit down in the chair to ponder this sudden turn of events. I try to be aware of my breath, but notice I'm not breathing. I inhale deeply to make sure I'm still alive. I exhale and ask myself, what happened? What caused me to feel this way?

I look at the situation. I'm discouraged because Jean seemed to brush me off very quickly. I apparently wanted more of her time, understanding and maybe comfort. I had called with expectations that I didn't even realize at the time. But, when the conversation didn't proceed the way I wanted it to, I reacted the same way I have for years.

I don't like the picture I see so I head back to the phone and call Jean again. This time she answers.

"Hello. . . ."

"Jean, this is Alan. I just called to apologize. I'm sorry that I reacted the way I did."

"Thank you," she says, "I know making this call was difficult and I appreciate the fact you did it."

"Please call me when you have some time. Okay?"

"I will." She pauses, "I definitely will. Thank you."

We hang up and I feel better. This is probably the first time in my life that I was aware of something *as* it happened. A situation like this would normally upset me for weeks. But this time I dealt with it. I believe Jean is a good influence. She's encouraging me to eat better and is somehow helping me look at myself and change. As a reward for this hard work, I decide to treat myself to doughnuts on the boardwalk and to relax. This is enough self-understanding for today.

10.

I walk on the boardwalk, get a doughnut with sprinkles, and head for the benches facing the ocean. I sit down and think. What an amazing eight hours. I hear voices in the night, have my first quarrel with Jean, and make up.

Without looking at my watch, I know it's noon because the seating arrangement is changing. The afternoon group is replacing the morning one.

This also reminds me it's time for pizza. I decide the doughnut was an appetizer and go to Angelo's. I eat three slices of pizza and drink a Pepsi. Once again I consider sitting here and watching the ocean for another four hours so I can order more pizza for dinner. I pry myself from the seat and walk out into the bright sun. The thought of a computer pops into my head. I forgot that I wanted to buy one today.

I head for Ashbury Street, the center of town, because I know there must be an electronics store there somewhere. I probably should read articles about which computer is best and shop for a good price. If I don't, the salesperson will sell me the one that earns the biggest commission. I meander along the street and within a block see a store and walk in.

"May I help you?" a clerk asks.

"I'm looking for a laptop computer," I say.

"Any particular model?"

"Well, I've been looking around a little and I like the Toshiba." That's not completely true, but I did see an advertisement in an airline magazine the last time I flew to California. That's looking around a little.

"Toshiba's my favorite," he says.

I'm not surprised.

He explains the features of the Toshiba and compares it to some other models. I like everything he's saying. Next he shows me a newspaper advertisement: "All Toshiba laptop computers, twenty percent off, software bundle included." And today is the last day of the sale.

I use the display model to type a few sentences. I like the feel of the keyboard. It seems like a good deal so I buy it. I do some fast calculating, and decide I can now live about nine months instead of a year without working. At home I take the computer out of the box, push and plug in some cords and turn it on. Up comes Windows. I click on Word and begin typing, "It was always the worst of times."

I wait all day to hear from Jean but don't. This both disturbs and relieves me. I want to be with her, but I don't want to be with her if she doesn't want to be with me. Although these thoughts distract me, I work on my book the remainder of the afternoon.

Around six P.M. I give up waiting for her to call and walk on the boardwalk to get some dinner. I order spaghetti at a restaurant where I can sit and watch the people. After I finish eating, I stroll to the far end of the boardwalk, past the condominiums, and sit on a bench at 2nd Street. Very few people are up here because there aren't any stores. I decide to be daring and sit on the lifeguard's chair on the beach. I did this once when I was sixteen. I wonder if the Ocean City Beach Patrol would arrest me.

I take off my shoes, walk out to the chair and climb up. As the anxiety subsides, I think about my breathing. It's short and shallow. The worst that can happen is that someone will tell me to leave. I relax a little, take deeper breaths, and watch the ocean. The only sound is a wave crashing onto the rocks. The sky is dark except for a trace of the moon. I stare at wave after wave, wondering if the woman in France is doing the same. Is she lonely? Is her friend busy tonight? Is she writing a book? Has she found the answers about the meaning of life?

I know I haven't fallen asleep, but I know a lot of time has elapsed. My breathing unites with the ocean. The separation between ocean and me disappears. Sometimes I think I become the ocean. I am the ebb and flow of the waves. I feel refreshed and calm.

As I head back to the boardwalk, I think about Jean. It would have been a different evening with her. We would have talked and maybe even held hands. But I wouldn't have been alone. I need that too. It restores something deep within me. Maybe she needs it too.

I open the door to the apartment and automatically look at the phone to see if there are any messages. There are none, but that's probably because I don't have an answering machine. If someone had called, it would have been Jean. No one else knows I'm here. I debate whether to contact my son and daughter or some acquaintance to let them know I'm in New Jersey.

"New Jersey?" they'd say. "Why New Jersey?"

And I wouldn't know how to answer them. Maybe I won't call. I'll wait to see how long I stay.

I go upstairs and get ready for bed. A thought flashes through my mind. Will I hear another strange voice tonight? I shrug off the idea but turn on a relaxation tape to lull me to sleep, just in case.

I wake up startled again. I know the same thing has happened. What did the voice say this time? Journey, something about a journey. I lie back and wait. The message comes again as if it's rising from inside me, swells and fills the room. "You are about to be taken on a journey of great proportions." I sit up, half-awake, blinking. Where is this coming from? What journey? Where am I going?

I decide to write this down. I fumble my way to the bureau, turn on a light and write, "You are about to be taken on a journey of great proportions."

Looking at the sentences from last night and tonight, I wonder if this is an omen or something.

For a few minutes I stand still. Although I know I'm alone in the room, I don't feel alone. I look around and peek out into the hallway. My first thought is to call Jean. My second thought is to get a glass of water. I go with the second one. There are no lights on in any of the houses around me. Everything's quiet. I think about walking over to the beach but decide it's too late. I'll try sleeping again even though I'm wide awake.

I turn on my Walkman, fold the pillow in half and stick it under my neck, a technique I discovered in my "worry" days when I used to lie awake for hours in the middle of the night running the store, paying the bills and figuring out budgets. Sticking pillows under my neck allowed me to sleep. I wasn't sure why it worked, but I surmised that it cut off the circulation of blood to my brain, like having an arm or leg fall asleep.

11.

The next time I open my eyes the room is filled with sunlight. I roll over and look at the clock. 9:30 A.M. Good. That makes the day shorter. I do some mental calculations. If I take an hour to shower and dress and a half-hour for breakfast, it will be almost lunch time. If I use the steamer for lunch, eat and clean up, it will be almost dinner time. If I use the steamer for dinner, eat and clean up, it will be almost time for bed. Ergo, if the only reason to get out of bed is to eat, I can skip that and stay in bed. I convince myself to stay in bed.

I lie here trying to enjoy not working, but it's not working. I'm not enjoying not working. I decide to counsel myself.

Okay, I say, what do you like to do?
Nothing really.
Try harder.
I like sitting and looking at the ocean.
Okay, and . . . ?
I like writing.
Then write your book about enlightenment.
But I'm not enlightened.
Do you like doing anything else?
I like reading.

There. You haven't read a book since you've been here. Today you can go and buy some books. So get out of bed and get going.

I lie in bed and think about this idea some more. I could take a book along with me to the boardwalk and read. That would be interesting. Okay. I'll buy some books.

It takes me an hour to shower, get dressed and eat breakfast which consists of my recently-purchased cereal and bread. I look at the clock and decide it's almost lunch time. As I walk to the bookstore, I argue with myself the whole way. The pivotal point of my rationalization is that I won't have time to make lunch before it's time for dinner.

I walk into the store and head for the humor section where I immediately find some old favorites such as Calvin and Hobbes. Laughing aloud, I discover that several children are staring at me. I get the impression they think I'm too old to read this, so I put the books back. Browsing in other sections, I find Emerson's essays, Thoreau's *Walden*, plus dozens of books on metaphysics, philosophy, psychology and psychotherapy. I purchase enough to fill a shopping bag.

On the way back to the apartment I can't decide if I should get pizza for lunch or go back and use the steamer to make rice and vegetables. I picture the vegetables deteriorating in my refrigerator and feel guilty. I go with the steamer.

I eat rice, vegetables and tofu, the only meal I know how to make. After everything is cleaned up and put away, I'm satisfied. I head for the living room and my stack of books. On top is *Walden*, and I decide it's a great place to start. I read it in college and always

Motorcycle Enlightenment

remembered the words, "Simplify, simplify, simplify." I wanted to follow that philosophy.

After reading for about an hour, I fall asleep with the book in my hands. A little later I wake up and read again. This pattern continues for most of the day.

Dinner means simply heating the other half of lunch in the microwave and eating it. The rest of the evening is a continuation of reading and sleeping. Finally around eleven P.M. I go upstairs. I've heard people say they can't take naps before going to bed. I, on the other hand, think of evening naps as one of the preliminary exercises for enjoying real sleep.

As I crawl into bed, I wonder if I'll be awakened at two A.M. again. I look for my notebook and pen and lay them on the floor beside the bed. I gaze around the room to see if I'm alone. For extra measure I tuck the pillow under my neck and hope that sleep comes quickly.

12.

I sit up in bed. My breath is short and rapid. A noise outside shatters the stillness. I leap out of bed and run down the steps. Jean's business card with her home telephone number is lying beside the phone. I dial her number and glance at the living room clock. It's two A.M.

A sleepy voice answers, "Hello."

"Jean, this is Alan."

Detecting my emotion she asks, "What's wrong?"

"I'm scared to death," I tell her.

"Should I come over?"

"No, but will you stay on the phone?"

"Sure, Alan. Take some deep breaths." She pauses. "Where are you?"

I look around. "I'm leaning against the stove in the kitchen."

"Why don't you go into the living room, sit down and tell me what's wrong?" she suggests.

I turn on every light as I go. I can hear my mother saying, "What do you think this is, Grand Central Station?" I never knew what that meant, but the thought makes me smile.

"Jean, I just had the most astonishing dream."

"What was it?"

"Well," I start, "it's so vivid, even now. It was in an office with rows of desks. I was at the front leaning back against a desk. I remember noticing the rolled-up cuffs of my long sleeve shirt. Several women and one man were sitting at their desks facing me. The man leaned forward and laughed while he said something like, 'That could never happen to you.' I have the idea that I was extremely wealthy, powerful and above anything happening *to* me.

"I remember suddenly yelling, 'That is not right, That is not right.'

"The scene instantly changed to a large, white, open convertible limousine where I was sitting on the back ledge like they do in parades. We were headed toward a stadium where I think I was going to be the speaker. Out of nowhere a huge arm grabbed me out of the car and dashed me to the ground. I know I died instantly." I take a deep sigh. "That's it."

I can hear Jean breathing. "Did you wake up at that moment?"

"Precisely at that moment," I tell her. "I hit the ground and woke up."

"How do you feel now?"

"Much better since talking to you. I think I'm okay. In fact, I should let you get back to sleep. I'll write it down while it's still fresh in my mind. Will you be able to sleep?"

"Certainly," she says to relieve my worry. "Are you sure you're okay? I could come over if you want."

"No, Jean, really, I'm alright now. But I can't tell you how much I appreciate being able to call you. Thanks. Goodnight."

I think about going upstairs, but know I'm not ready

to return to the bedroom. I remember my computer and decide to type the details in a file called "Dream." About three A.M., I turn off all the lights and head upstairs, although I'm still a little reluctant to go into the bedroom. For the second time tonight I get into bed quickly, tuck the pillow behind my neck and hope to fall asleep.

13.

I wake up around 9:00 A.M. and the phone rings. I run downstairs and, at about the third step I think, this is a cordless phone. Why don't I take it upstairs with me at night?

I pick up the phone and say, "Hello."

"Hi, Alan. It's Jean. How are you this morning?"

"I just woke up," I tell her, "but I think I'm okay." I look down to see if my body is still here. "Yeah, I'm fine."

"You scared me last night."

"I scared myself, too."

"Would you like to go out for dinner tonight?" she asks.

"I'd love to," I reply, "and I really mean that."

"Great, see you around six-thirty."

At 6:30 P.M. I look at my watch and know she's not coming. She got tied up at work, can't get away and won't make it. I pace around the house and look out every window at least ten times. Where is she? Now I'm both worried and upset.

At 6:42 she pulls up.

I greet her at the sidewalk with less enthusiasm than I had planned all day. She senses it and asks, "What's wrong?"

"I thought you weren't coming."

She looks at her watch. "It's six-thirty-five."

"Six-forty-two," I correct her.

"Alan," she says, "I run on 'ish' time."

I look at her in bewilderment. "Ish time? What's that?"

"You know, six-thirty-ish, seven-ish." She smiles and laughs.

I see no humor in it and explain to her, "I'm never late, period. For instance, if I had a two-forty-five dental appointment and something interrupted my schedule, I would drive seventy miles an hour to be there on time even though I knew the dentist always ran late and wouldn't take me before three. It's just the way I am. When I have an appointment, I plan my whole day around it and arrive at least fifteen minutes early. Sometimes I even drive around the block four or five times, although," I add parenthetically, "I never venture too far away because I might get lost."

"I'm sorry," she says, "I didn't realize you were so obsessed with time."

"Well, I am. But in spite of that I'm very glad you're here."

"Thank you," she replies and asks, "How are you?"

"Fine," I answer. "Want to come in?"

"Actually I'm really hungry. Are you ready to go?"

There's no way I'm telling her that I looked at my watch every fifteen minutes since two and was ready to go at five. "Yes, I'm ready," I say and open the car door.

She senses my discomfort, reaches over and pats my hand.

"I heard it," she says. "I heard that heart crack open a little bit."

This brings a smile. "Yeah," I agree, "I felt it too."

In the restaurant she asks, "Would you like to discuss your dream?"

"There's nothing more to say. After talking with you I calmed down and wrote about it in the computer."

"You got the computer?"

I forgot she hadn't seen it. "Yeah. Now I can tell everyone I'm doing freelance writing. That's an occupation and so I'm working again. Not fast or hard, but working."

"Good for you."

She's so encouraging I actually feel proud.

Returning to the dream she asks, "What do you think it means?"

"I don't know, honestly. I didn't give any thought to analyzing it. What do you think?"

"I suspect that you were releasing some strong beliefs you held about yourself. The reason the arm came out of nowhere was because it was your own arm. Our dreams allow us to examine ourselves, try out new perspectives and experiment with choices. I wonder if the you who wanted businesses, money and power is dissolving. That's why you said, 'It's not right.' You consciously made the decision that you want to change."

"I hadn't thought about it that way, but I like it. And, truthfully, it makes sense. The more I'm away from the businesses, the more I don't want to go back."

"Alan," she says, "there's a you behind those eyes that I know very well. And he's starting to emerge."

After dinner we go back to the apartment to see the computer.

She notices my pile of books on the kitchen table and asks, "Did you just buy these?"

"Yeah, why?"

"Interesting timing. You buy the computer to write, books for inspiration, and you have the dream."

Jean likes my new computer. I tell her I used to own three because I had a theory: "If one doesn't make you happy, two will. And if two don't, three surely will. I called it Alan's Law."

Jean winces at this logic.

I show her the file on the dream and a few pages of my book, but I don't want her to read too much. When the time is right, I'll ask for her opinion. She doesn't object, so I turn off the computer.

14.

A few minutes later we're sitting together on the couch. I put my arm around her and pull her closer. "I like this part the best," I tell Jean.

"This is the tightwire," she says. "If we can walk it straight, it's okay. Too much movement either to the right or the left and we lose our balance."

I sense her seriousness and walk it straight.

A little later she says, "I was just remembering Stuart Crawley's chocolate ice cream cone theory and how he enjoyed sharing it with others. I found it helpful and I'd like to tell you if you won't be offended."

This immediately makes me nervous, but I assure her I won't be offended. Actually, I can't promise I won't be but I want to hear it.

"Once there was a young boy who desired the perfect, chocolate ice cream cone. Each time he got a cone he was sure that this one would be it but it never was. Sometimes the cone was stale. Sometimes the ice cream was too soft and melted on his clothes. One time the ice cream fell right out of the cone onto the sidewalk and he cried. You name it and it happened. So each time he thought about this perfect cone he added more qualifications to the list: perfect taste, perfect cone, perfect everything. Then one day he realized this could go on forever and he decided that he wasn't going to search for the perfect cone any longer. He was just going to enjoy each one as it was."

"Good for him," I say.

She continues. "Many people, according to Stuart, spend their lives searching for the perfect ice cream cone. But life isn't like that. There is no one perfect cone. Each one is different and equally enjoyable in its own way."

I think I understand the story," I say. "I've always been searching for that cone, figuratively speaking. I hadn't thought of it in those terms, but I'm sure that's right."

"Okay," she says, "although it might be presumptuous of me, that's what I've been a little worried about recently. I don't want you to think that I'm your perfect ice cream cone. It would be wonderful if this turns out to be an ideal relationship. If it happens—great. But . . ."

I frown.

She looks at me.

I sit and stare out the window.

"I was really hurt when my marriage ended," she explains, "so I've been very careful about any relationships."

"Fine," I say, disheartened.

We sit quietly for awhile. She doesn't talk and I'm afraid to move.

Jean stands up. "I better go. It's getting late."

"Okay."

"Don't get up," she says.

I listen and don't move.

She says goodnight as she closes the door.

I look at the wall and reflect. The perfect, chocolate ice cream cone. She might be right. Maybe that's what I've been doing.

15.

I wake up panting and scared because I know I died in my dream again. I lie back and breathe deeply to recall the events. This dream took place at the store I used to own. I was riding my motorcycle in the garage, but somehow was not going anywhere. Suddenly the motorcycle turned 180 degrees, accelerated, and smashed into the wall. This is when I woke up. I reach down and pick up the notebook, which I left lying beside the bed, and write down the details.

Unable to sleep, I try analyzing the dream as Jean did. Surely it's telling me something. All my life I've been running and searching for, I hesitate to say, the perfect ice cream cone. And where has it gotten me? I conclude that the dream is basic. If I keep running blindly, one day I'll hit a brick wall and die as confused as I am now.

16.

I wake up and feel refreshed. For me, this is an unusual response. Normally I cover my head and tell the morning to go away. But today I feel like getting out of bed and making the day worthwhile. I touch my forehead to see if I have a fever.

As I'm showering, I decide a little more normalcy would be beneficial in my life. From somewhere, I come up with the idea of writing my chores on three-by-five cards. I think more about the idea as I eat toast with almond butter. I decide to walk to the store on the corner, buy the cards, and organize my life.

On one card I write "Do laundry;" on another, "Clean bathroom;" on another, "Pay bills;" on another, "Contact family," and so on, until I have twenty-five cards. Each evening I will look over the cards, plan what I need to do the following day and put those cards in a separate pile. When I finish a task, I'll date the card and return it to the stack.

I feel so elated with this idea that I select the "Do laundry" card first. I gather my dirty clothes, put them in a plastic bag and head for the laundromat which I noticed and avoided several times already. I didn't bother to tell Jean that I was paying to have my clothes

Motorcycle Enlightenment

washed at the dry cleaners. Although I'm anxious, I know it can't be that difficult.

I take a deep breath as I walk in. No one is here: good and bad. No one will know this is my first time, but, no one is here to help if I get stuck. I spot a change machine, take out a dollar and put it in. The dollar comes back. My stomach knots. Even little setbacks trouble me. I study the diagram on the machine and see that I inserted the dollar upside down. I try again. Out come four quarters. Yes!

Next I need detergent. I should have bought this at the store where it's cheaper, but I console myself by remembering this is my first time, on the spur of the moment. I put a dollar in and get a small packet of detergent. Things are going smoothly.

I take all my dirty laundry—shirts, jeans, dish towels, everything—and put them into one machine. I dump in the detergent, line up the quarters in the slots and push them in. The machine starts. I look around with pride but no one sees me which is probably better anyway.

There's a reason why I never did a load of wash. All my life people have taken care of me and done my work. First it was my mother, then it was my wife. When we divorced and I moved into an apartment, I hired a cleaning lady who did my wash. As for meals, assuming I ate twenty-one a week, at least twelve were in restaurants. The rest were cold cereal breakfasts or prepared foods. Even if I started a project on my own, someone usually appeared out of nowhere and completed it for me. At Christmas, the only time during the year when I shopped, I would walk into a store and look around. No matter how busy the store was, a clerk would immediately appear and ask if I needed help. From that point on, I followed him around the store as he did my shopping for me. Often one salesclerk took care of all the presents I had to buy.

The washer stops, which reminds me I need to get more change for the dryer. Putting the dollar bill in the machine the right way on the first try and getting four quarters in return is blissful. I open the dryer door, take each piece of laundry out of the washer and throw it across the room into the dryer. I put in enough quarters for thirty minutes—just a guess—and push the button. It starts. This pleases me immensely.

Thirty minutes later the dryer stops and the lack of noise startles me. I look up from the book I'm reading and realize I'm still in the laundromat. After a few moments to orient myself, I smooth out my laundered jeans and shirts and fold them neatly. The rest of the clothes I put in the bag. I walk out of the laundromat with a sense of satisfaction.

Back at the apartment I put the laundry away, get the three-by-five card marked "Do laundry," write today's date on it, and reinsert it in the stack.

Next I sit down and write short letters to my son and daughter. Basically the letters say the same thing: "I'm doing okay. I'm temporarily living in New Jersey. I hope everything's going well for you."

Now at least they know I'm alive.

Not wanting to overdo this new work ethic, I add a few more cards: Walk on the boardwalk. Get pizza. Eat doughnuts.

I can't believe I made breakfast and did the laundry already. Now I start rice in the steamer for lunch. Chores like these were never my forte, but give me a business and I'll have it running smoothly and accurately. Maybe that's my part in the scheme of things.

Motorcycle Enlightenment

I finish lunch, put everything away and add a "Reading books" card to the stack. Then I sit down and read *Walden*. Thoreau writes: "It is not all books that are as dull as their readers. There are probably words addressed to our condition exactly, which, if we could really hear and understand, would be more salutary than the morning or the spring to our lives, and possibly put a new aspect on the face of things for us. How many a man has dated a new era in his life from the reading of a book!"

Interesting. Why would I have dreams several nights in a row? Why would I wake up so alive and ready to begin a new life this morning? Why would I read that sentence on p. 77? (Always my lucky number.) "Alan," I tell myself, "I think you're about to begin a new era in your life."

I read more of Thoreau. "The book exists for us, perchance, which will explain our miracles and reveal new ones. The at present unutterable things we may find somewhere uttered. These same questions that disturb and puzzle and confound us have in their turn occurred to all the wise men; not one has been omitted; and each has answered them, according to his ability, by his words and his life."

My heart is racing. Why *this* page on *this* day? Is it possible that my questions will be answered? Is it possible that I will answer them by *my* words and life?

I want to call Jean and read the page to her but decide against it. I read for about an hour and fall asleep—still my greatest talent. I wake up feeling relaxed. Since today is the first day of my card file and I can organize it any way I want, I put "Walk on beach" on top.

When I go upstairs to get the house key, I check my appearance in the mirror and notice that I'm wearing a long sleeve shirt. I'll have to think about wearing tennis shorts and a teeshirt the next time.

I walk on the sand, just out of reach of the water. I'm not anxious about anything. I feel light. I don't know how to describe it. I know, for instance, that if I sat down on a beach chair to watch the ocean right now, the person next to me wouldn't turn on a radio.

I walk a sensible distance, turn around and come back. The walk is invigorating. I sit on the steps of the boardwalk and let my mind play its usual game—pizza or steamer, steamer or pizza. Where do these thoughts come from? I'm not wearing my watch so I don't know if it's time to eat. It probably is. But what was it that caused that particular thought to jump into my head at that particular moment? Maybe it was the scent of pizza wafting towards me. I like the idea of eating pizza and convince myself I deserve it because I had a good day. I agree with myself and eat pizza for dinner.

17.

"Hello." I hear a sleepy voice say. "Hello, who is it?"
"It's me, Alan, I think."
The voice gets clearer and stronger. "Alan, what's wrong?"
"I'm not sure. I don't remember calling you, exactly. What time is it?"
"About three A.M." Jean says. "Where are you?"
In somewhat of a stupor I look around and answer, "In the kitchen."
"What are you doing?" she asks.
I look down at my feet and tell her the feet I see aren't mine. She starts to laugh and restrains herself. "Whose feet are they?"
"I don't know," I answer seriously, "I think an elephant's." I stomp on the floor loudly so she can hear the noise. "Hear that?"
"I hear you stomping on the floor. Alan, I think I better come right over."
"No. Just talk to me. I'm coming back slowly."
"Where were you?"
"I don't know."
I look at my hands and they seem extra large. I now remember that I had difficulty dialing the telephone. I

pushed two and three buttons at a time. "My hands are real big, Jean."

"Oh," she says, not wanting to show concern and worry me. She waits a long time. "Are you back now?"

I look over my body and take a few deep breaths. "Yes, I'm me."

Jean speaks calmly. "Alan, apparently you stayed in the dream state for awhile after part of you awakened. What do you think?"

"Maybe."

"Are you better now?"

"Yes, much better. Thanks."

"Would you like me to come over?"

"Sure," I say, with my usual enthusiasm.

"Because you're scared or worried," she adds.

"Oh. No, I think I'm okay now."

"I can tell."

"Thank you, Jean. I don't know what I'd do without you. But I promise, no more calls in the middle of the night."

"It's okay, Alan. Just as long as you're alright."

"I am, thanks, goodnight."

I hang up and head for the computer. This event gets typed in a file called "Real Big."

Jean calls in the morning to check on me. "How are you doing now?"

Feeling embarrassed I answer, "Fine, thanks. I promise not to call you anymore in the middle of the night." I feel silly and don't know what else to say.

Jean realizes this and changes the subject. "Unfortunately," she says, "I'm busy the rest of the week, but hopefully we can get together over the weekend. How does that sound?"

Motorcycle Enlightenment

"Far away," I answer honestly. "Let me know."

"I will," she says cheerily. "Goodbye."

I hang up and make a depressed face in the mirror. There you go again, says a voice inside. Chase after happiness and run away from sadness. Step back and see that the two are one.

Two are one? It reminds me of an e e cummings poem that says, "twice two makes five is sometimes a very charming thing too." But I've always tried to make twice two equal four. It's logical and controlled, but maybe not so charming.

18.

As the week passes my life falls into a pattern because the cards work wonderfully. My clothes and house are clean and I feel healthier. I make new cards: "Stretching exercises" and "Whatever needs to be done." I worry that I might be getting carried away with this idea when I make a "Cut fingernails" card.

I now have forty cards and do three each day. I sleep through the night, spend time on the beach and boardwalk, and make progress in my reading and writing. I even get return letters from Emily and Mark. All in all, I'm doing well. I'm still living from savings and haven't added a penny of income, but I'm not worrying too much because I'm okay for several more months.

Jean calls and asks if I'm free tomorrow. Of course I am. But I get so excited about wanting to see her tomorrow that I decide to skip today. So instead of following the cards as I had laid them out, I arrange them in a new order. Spontaneity is also good I tell myself.

Time is certainly relative. I could have figured out that theory by myself, but without all the equations. When I'm enjoying "my time," twenty four hours is too short for one day. When I'm not doing what I want, or

Motorcycle Enlightenment

waiting for something I do want, I call it "work time" and each minute seems like twenty four hours.

Today is running on "work time." My left arm hurts. My rotator cuff, I decide. I attribute this pain to the fact that I've been looking at my watch all day trying to make time go faster. I don't know where my rotator cuff is, but it seems like the right body part since I wear my watch at the cuff of my shirt, and I've been rotating my wrist all day to see what time it is.

Around 8:30 P.M. I go to bed. My rationalization is that the earlier I go to bed, the faster morning will come so I can get up.

At 4:30 A.M. I wake up. I know I'm having another dream, but I can't remember it entirely. It seems as if the end of the Earth was involved. I know Jean and I were together. I'm not sure where it was taking place, but I remember being in the foreground when a strange lady came into the scene. She was dark-haired and had a symbol on the front of her. She lay down as if she were signaling the end of the world. Suddenly a figure of an Egyptian, like a pharaoh, sat up and bellowed, "No!" Then everything changed and all kinds of wavy lines and symbols began passing in front of him. It was almost as if his roaring "No" was so loud it shook the earth. Strange bright symbols continued in front of him as he yelled.

I reach for my notebook and write down the details. Momentarily I think about getting up and typing in the computer since I've already had eight hours of sleep. But I remind myself that this would make the morning six hours longer before Jean arrives. I roll over and go back to sleep. I wake up again at 8:30. Only two hours and she'll be here. This relative time system really works.

19.

It's 10:35 A.M., but I don't panic because I know Jean will arrive on "ish" time as usual. Sure enough, ten-thirty-ish for her, 10:42 and thirty seconds for me, she pulls up. I'm sitting on the small porch pretending to read and not notice her.

"Anyone home?" she says, tapping on my book.

I look up. "Is it ten-thirty already?" I stand up and hug Jean.

"That's a nice greeting."

"Well, I missed you."

"Thanks," she says. "So, what are we doing today?"

"I don't know. I hadn't thought about it."

"I suppose that means you didn't pack any lunch or dinner?"

"Hadn't thought about eating," I confess.

"What were you thinking about?"

"Seeing you. I didn't get any further than that."

"Well, fortunately I did. Are you ready for an adventure?"

"You know me. Anything spontaneous."

She smiles. "I'll bet you even have a card that says 'Relax.'"

I know she peeked in my stack.

Motorcycle Enlightenment

As we get into the car, I glance in the backseat and see a cooler and basket. "I'm glad you planned today."

"Me too," she agrees. "I knew if I didn't, we might end up with your suggestion."

"And what would that have been?"

"You greet me with a dozen red roses as I arrive precisely on time. Then you suggest that we ride bikes on the boardwalk, eat doughnuts, walk on the boardwalk, eat pizza, sit on the benches, read, eat more pizza, walk on the beach, and go home."

"What a great day."

"That's what you do almost every day."

"I have great days every day."

We drive out of Ocean City.

"Lost?" Jean asks.

"Since we crossed the 9th Street bridge."

"You'll like where we're going," she says but doesn't tell me where we're going.

We drive up Route 9, turn on 72 and go out on Long Beach. The sign indicates Barnegat Lighthouse. She pulls into the lot, parks and looks at me. "Like it?"

"Yes. How did you know I like lighthouses?"

"Just a guess," she replies.

"I used to fantasize about living in one."

Jean touches me on the arm. "Let's go over."

We walk to the lighthouse and explore the surrounding area. After awhile we look for a spot to put down our blanket and have lunch. When we find the perfect place, I tell her gallantly, "I'll save it while you get the lunch out of the car."

"Thanks," she says, "but I need your brawn."

"Brain?" I question.

"Brawn," she corrects. "It's your brain that gets you in such a dither."

We finish eating, put the leftovers in the cooler, and stretch out on the blanket. We watch white puffy clouds float in the sky behind the lighthouse. Simultaneously we experience the same effect.

"The lighthouse is moving," she says.

"I know. Doesn't it feel as if the land is moving and the clouds are standing still?"

"Exactly," she agrees.

Without a reference point on the ground, it seems as if there is no way of knowing which is actually moving, the lighthouse or the clouds. We enjoy the sensation.

"The lighthouse is moving and not moving," she says.

"That's impossible," I correct her. "It can't do both."

"Yes it can," she counters. "What is the lighthouse made of?"

"Cement?"

"Smaller."

"Chunks of cement?"

"No. What is everything made of?"

"I don't know. Maybe atoms or molecules. Energy?"

"And what is that characteristic?"

"Movement," I say, realizing her intent. "So the lighthouse doesn't physically move, but its very essence is energy which is constantly moving."

I continue watching from this new perspective.

"My time" goes by too quickly. We repack the cooler, since I snacked while we watched the clouds, and fold the blanket.

Back at the car she asks, "Will you drive home?"

"Uh," I say, "if . . ."

She finishes. "If I stay awake until you know where you are?"

Motorcycle Enlightenment

I hesitate to tell her that will be 9th Street in Ocean City. One trip on unfamiliar roads is useless. "Sure."

She guides me out to Route 9, reclines her seat slightly, and closes her eyes. "Will you be okay if I rest for awhile?"

"Of course," I say, not caring if I get lost and drive like this forever.

"I mean," she corrects, "can you get us home okay?"

"Oh. I have no idea. You just rest and I'll be fine."

She knows I can't stray too far from home if I stay on Route 9.

My mind starts up. Energy. Moving/Not moving. Up/Down. Happiness/Suffering. Perceptions. The lighthouse wasn't moving, but, from my perspective, it appeared to be moving. So, at that moment what appeared to be real wasn't real. In a sense I was creating reality. A dump truck of thoughts fall on me. Suppose my thoughts create my reality. Maybe things are just as they are and I decide the meaning. There's a multitude of data available in the world, but I only see what I want to see based on what I expect to see. And what I expect to see is basically a repeat of past experiences which, in a sense, are determining my future.

Jean wakes up, sees a sign for Cape May and asks, "Lost?"

I'm totally absorbed in my thinking. I look around and notice I'm driving. "At least we're safe," I answer proudly.

"Yes," she agrees, "but you missed the turn to Ocean City. We're on our way to Cape May."

"And we can't do that today because you have to go home."

"Right," she says.

I turn right at the next street.

After turning around in a driveway, I take a left back onto Route 9.

"Just missed some signs for the bridge into Ocean City. Thinking?" she asks.

"Thinking," I nod.

"Thought so."

"Thought right," I answer and turn right at the sign that says Ocean City.

Jean thanks me for driving home and gives me a kiss.

"I had a lovely day," she says.

"Me too."

"I couldn't have planned it better myself," she adds with a smile.

20.

I continue my routine of living according to the suggestions on the three-by-five cards, plus spending a lot of time thinking about perceptions. The lighthouse really did feel as if it were moving, but that, I realize, was just how I perceived it at that moment. This leads me to think that everything is relative and exists according to who is perceiving it. What I think is true is only my belief, my perception of reality. I find it fascinating that people have their own beliefs and see the world through the reality they generate.

I spend hours sitting, thinking and writing. For a diversion I head up to the boardwalk for a stroll. I see the doughnut shop and buy a multi-colored, sprinkled doughnut. I walk for several blocks as I continue thinking and then remember that I want to sit and eat my doughnut, but it's gone. I realize what happened. I already ate the doughnut. How disappointing.

I stop walking, and for the first time, understand what just occurred—the part of me that I consider "me" wasn't aware of what another part of me was doing. Suddenly this seems *very* important.

I return to the store and buy another doughnut, sit on a bench and concentrate on enjoying each bite. This time

I finish the doughnut with pleasure and lick the last morsel from my fingers.

What was the difference between eating the first doughnut and the second? Awareness of the moment is critical. If I'm not paying attention, something takes over my body and runs on automatic pilot. I don't actually know where "I" go, but I do know that in this instance an "I—a Doughnut I"—ate my first doughnut.

The "I" that I think I am was lost in thought. This "I—a Nondoughnut I"—suddenly became aware of the situation.

I think I'm on to something. I begin strolling on the boardwalk and think about this more. Eventually I stop to see where I am but I'm not sure. The boardwalk is two and a half miles from beginning to end, but only a portion of that distance has stores. I've gone past all the stores hundreds of times and still have no idea of their relative position to one another. For instance, I never remember if the movie theaters are above or below 9th Street, and I don't know where the bike rental is in relation to Angelo's Pizza. This leads to another realization. I'm not very observant.

Though I'm not certain where I am at the moment, I do know that I need to write down this information about "awareness." I go into a store and purchase a notebook and pen that fit in my shirt pocket. At the rail on the boardwalk I write: "Doughnut I. Nondoughnut I. Awareness."

I continue walking, absorbed in my thoughts, but feel that something isn't right. I stop, look around and discover that I'm no longer on the boardwalk. Where am I going? Why? I know some stray thought beamed into my head and I responded to it without question.

Motorcycle Enlightenment

I try not to think about anything other than inhaling and exhaling. I take in a deep breath and concentrate on the air coming into my nostrils. Jean taught me how to breathe deeply into my abdomen so I try to feel the air filling my body. I hold it momentarily and slowly exhale, feeling the air leave my nostrils. "I wonder," pops into my mind, but I stop it before it gets too far and immediately go back to the inhalation. In a matter of ten seconds I see a battle going on between myself and myself. If I'm the one who wants to be calm and breathe, who wants to think all these thoughts? Am I the person trying to be calm? Am I the person thinking? Am I the person observing all of this? Which I am I?

21.

After lunch I head for the computer. I label a file "Awareness." As I begin writing I come to my first realization: I don't know who I am. I know a part of me spends a lot of time thinking while another part of me functions automatically. And I know that another part of me is beginning to observe this. But how is all that possible? How can I do something when I'm not aware that I'm doing it?

I consider. I know my heart beats without my conscious involvement and that system works well. And there are also numerous other bodily activities that go on without my intervention. I suppose that's okay. But, I also know that I often walk, talk, eat and drive without awareness. Doing these activities mechanically concerns me. If I'm not doing them, who is?

I try to logically analyze this. I know that I perceive the world through my five senses and the information I receive is sorted, filed and stored in my brain, or somewhere. I imagine my head as an attic with stacks of boxes labeled according to the thoughts that are in them. So, each moment my senses supply data to me and I respond to the information. I'd like to believe that I'm actually aware of what I'm doing and choosing my response in every situation.

Motorcycle Enlightenment

But my guess is the "Thinking I" is usually unaware of the moment and the robotic "Doughnut I" is in charge. I surmise that over the years it has become an efficient machine, categorizing situations and using the same responses over and over. So, in a sense, I have become these repeated patterns which have turned into crystallized habits. This realization leads me to wonder if there are actually grooves in my brain where these habitual thoughts travel. Viewing my life from this perspective, I understand that what I call the present is more a reliving of the past. But what is the past?

I suppose it's everything that has ever happened to me. And it's all stored in my head and retrieved by thinking about it. For instance, if I think about my former businesses, thoughts about their success appear which trigger good feelings about myself. I feel proud as a result. But, if I picture myself moving into the apartment after my divorce, failure thoughts overwhelm me and instantly I'm depressed.

All these memories are stuffed into my brain, then a catalyst comes along and activates them. They appear as thoughts and I think them. This in turn generates feelings which I try to suppress. While I'm doing this, the "Doughnut I" lives my life. I think I'm right about this.

I wonder if my future is also based on my past, and what I expect to happen is simply a projection of what has already happened. Possibly the Doughnut I prepares itself to meet the day by creating an imaginary picture of how it wants events to unfold and then sees only data that confirms it. That would mean my memories, the impressions stored in the boxes in my brain, are the basis for how I have coped with the world, am coping, and will cope. From this perspective the "outside world" is like modeling clay which I shape, trying to make life match my expectations.

This, I guess, is what makes up my personality. So when Jean says I'm doing something out of character, what she really means is that I have deviated from the tracks I normally follow. But because this so rarely happens, my patterns are predictable and "I" can navigate in the world without any real awareness. That doesn't leave much room for change except through real effort.

I get so excited with this as the puzzle pieces begin falling into place that I can't sit still. I head for the freezer, dish out a bowl of ice cream, cover it with Cool Whip and start eating. Try as I might, I can't concentrate on the dessert because the flow of thoughts is building. I finish the ice cream, rinse the bowl and find myself back at the computer. Maybe that's who I am: a storage box of past events that are continually recycled.

Every time I get a different thought, that's who I become. For instance, I walk past Angelo's, think about pizza, and suddenly I'm a "hungry I" who wants to eat. Or, I'm sitting quietly in a chair and a thought about money beams into my head and begins collecting similar ones. Soon I'm a "money I" engrossed in these thoughts and worrying about whether I can afford to stay in Ocean City.

This describes my life. I'm constantly bombarded by thoughts that swing me in one direction or another. From one moment to the next I never know what I'll be thinking or feeling. I don't think I like this approach to life.

22.

I look at the clock, see it's approaching dinner time, and decide to eat. It occurs to me that I wasn't hungry until I saw what time it was. I go into the kitchen, get out the steamer, and put water in the base. As I'm measuring the amount of rice to use, I recall the time Mrs. Crawley helped me prepare dinner for Jean. I remember how nervous I was about burning my fingers and then I burned them. I think about Jean's surprised look when she saw the food and how much fun that dinner was.

I stop, look at what I'm doing, and realize that I'm preparing broccoli. In my systematic way of doing things, that means I've already measured the rice and water, placed them in the steamer and turned it on. Apparently from the little practice I've had, I've learned this task well enough so that the "conscious I" has turned the chore over to the "mechanical I" so I could spend more time thinking. But this doesn't please me anymore. I want to live my life when it happens.

I concentrate on eating my meal and enjoying it. After cleaning up the dishes I head back to the computer. If I want to be more aware of each moment, what must I do differently?

For one, I need to notice when I start drifting and

following whatever thoughts are appearing. So, when a thought suddenly occurs, I must choose whether I wish to think it or not. If I don't want to think it, I have to force myself to focus on something else. I don't have to run back and forth like a pendulum whenever my thoughts change. I don't have to become the thought. This means I don't have to react to it either.

In Viktor Frankl's *Man's Search for Meaning*, he said that "Everything can be taken from a man but one thing: the last of the human freedoms—to choose one's attitude in any given set of circumstances, to choose one's own way." Is that the answer? As each thought presents itself, I can choose what I'm going to do with it. But, and this is a key, I can only choose how I'm going to respond if I'm aware that "I" am not the thought.

The phone rings, jolting me. I first look at the clock, see it's 9:30 P.M., and realize that I've been sitting at the computer for hours. I then wonder who would call at this hour but answer my own question. Of course it's Jean. Who else could it be?

"I'm going for a walk on the beach," she says. "Want to join me?"

It does sound appealing so I'll follow this thought.

"Sure, should I come over?"

"No. I'll be right there. Bye."

A few minutes later I meet Jean at the curb. She's in shorts and I'm wearing a coat. We go down the street, up the ramp, over the boardwalk, down the steps and out onto the beach. We stop and watch rapidly moving clouds expose a full moon.

"This is nice. Let's stay like this forever."

She looks at me quizzically and says, "You know..."

"Yes?" I say, not really wanting to know.

Motorcycle Enlightenment

"Everything changes."

I frown.

"That's the nature of energy. Remember Stuart Crawley's theory of the perfect ice cream cone?"

"Yes."

"Well, here it is in reverse."

"What do you mean?"

"Instead of searching for the perfect cone, you think you've already found it. And when you do, you want to keep it just the way it is without changing. It's impossible."

"And I thought this walk was a break from thinking."

Jean laughs and takes my hand. She tugs me into motion and begins walking toward the lifeguard's chair. We climb up and get comfortable.

"This is another perfect moment," I say.

"Exactly," she agrees, "and that's the point. Had you been able to solidify the previous moment, we couldn't have experienced this one."

"You're right, Jean. But that's what I always try to do."

She waits for me to explore this notion myself.

"Nothing is ever exactly the way I want it. So I keep searching. And, when I'm with you, I'm often as close as I can imagine so I want to freeze it in place forever."

"You mean you want to be eternally happy in that one moment?"

"Not exactly. I want to use it somehow to disappear."

I can tell she's recording this comment. "That's a big difference between us, Alan. I enjoy each moment. I like to feel and experience things."

"I guess I don't."

"I think I've learned that about you. And there's something you have to realize. I'm not the perfect solution to your life, and I won't be frozen into one moment for eternity."

23.

Days pass as I continue working with several ideas. I'm fascinated with the understanding that I am not my thoughts. I also ponder the notion that I've been searching for perfection and hoping to capture it. Today I decide to use Jean's approach and enjoy each moment as it comes. I take an early morning stroll, read and write, eat and nap. A knock on the door awakens me, but, for a few seconds, I have no idea where I am. A second knock propels me out of bed and to the door.

"Sleeping?" Jean asks.

"Resting," I reply.

There's an excitement in her voice. "I don't have to work today. Would you like to do something?"

"Sure. What?"

"Let's go for a ride on your motorcycle."

"You're kidding?"

"No, honestly. I'd love to."

I shake my head. "I only have one helmet."

A big smile beams across her face. "I already thought of that and borrowed one from a friend."

"Well, then, come in and I'll get ready." I run up the steps two at a time.

She calls up after me. "Just promise me you won't

Motorcycle Enlightenment

wear your leather jacket and boots." She laughs at the image she's created.

Upstairs I decide to turn the joke on her. I dig to the bottom of the clothes in the drawer and find my bathing suit. Next I take out my old, dark blue socks and wingtip shoes. I even take off my shirt to reveal an untanned stomach. I can't bare to look in the mirror.

"I'll be there in a minute," I call downstairs.

"Don't hurry," she says.

I'm not certain why I had this idea, but I bolster my courage and go down the steps.

Jean looks up. Her hands cover her mouth and I can tell she's making a sound but nothing is coming out. My first thought is I don't know CPR. Finally there's an audible laugh.

"I'm ready," I say.

This ignites her laughter. At occasional pauses she manages to utter, "I don't believe it! This is so out of character for you."

I'm enjoying the moment. "So you don't know everything about me, do you?"

Shaking her head. "Definitely not."

I hitch up my bathing suit so high the netting sticks out under the legs. "Let that be a lesson to you," I say in my best John Wayne imitation.

She half-sits, half-falls back onto the couch. "You're crazy."

"Thank you, Ma'am. Thank you very much." This time in my best Elvis Presley voice.

"Stop. I can't laugh anymore."

I head up the stairs, but stop after two steps to peek back at her. She's leaning back, shaking her head and laughing. This was more successful than I expected.

The next time I come down I'm wearing jeans and a long sleeve shirt. She looks at the shirt, rolls her eyes and reminds me, "It's eighty degrees."

"Yes," I agree, "but combined with the speed from the cycle the wind chill index makes it about seventy."

"That cold?"

This is going to be fun riding the motorcycle. I know I won't have any cramps or lose my wallet. Jean climbs on the back of the cycle and puts her arms around me. I use the electric start and carefully pull out of the driveway. Since I have no idea where we're going, we quickly develop a method of communication. When we come to a stop sign or light, Jean taps me on the shoulder for the direction I need to turn. No tap means go straight ahead.

After a few miles Jean taps me on my right shoulder, but there's no place to turn. I hear her laughing. "No," she yells. "Look in the sky."

A rainbow.

I glance back and forth between the rainbow and the road. "It's a sign," I yell.

"What?"

"Pretty."

She nods her head to let me know she heard me and smashes her face guard into my shoulder.

After forty-five minutes, Jean taps me on my left shoulder and I turn into the driveway of a Victorian bed-and-breakfast that has an adjoining restaurant. I park the motorcycle and we stretch our legs. Jean suggests we have dinner.

The hostess seats us at a window which overlooks a small lake. We have casual conversation about the motorcycle ride, the weather and her work. After dessert Jean says, "Do you know what, Alan?"

"No," I respond.

Motorcycle Enlightenment

"I don't have to work tomorrow."

"That's nice."

"I have an idea," she continues.

"Which is?" Sometimes conversations with Jean go this way. She leads me on with short introductions, slowly arriving at the point. I, on the other hand, would tell a stranger on the street every detail of my life if asked. But I enjoy Jean's approach.

"Let's get a room at the bed-and-breakfast. We can sit by the lake, and you can tell me about your latest ideas."

I'm a little shocked.

"Two beds," she says.

"Okay, that would be . . . interesting."

"I thought you'd be more excited."

"I'm surprised. I obviously don't have anything with me."

Smiling, Jean pulls out her shoulder bag. I wondered why she had it because she rarely carries anything with her. She takes out two toothbrushes, a disposable razor and shaving cream. She leans the bag in my direction so I can see pajamas inside.

"I don't believe you. You had this planned all along."

She laughs. "Let's pay the bill and go sit by the lake."

"We better check to see if they have a room."

"All done. I called yesterday."

I stare at Jean's beautiful smile. I enjoy being with her. She appreciates each moment. Maybe, someday, I will too. I like this one.

We walk beside the lake and sit down on a bench.

"So," she says, "tell me about your most recent mental explorations."

I laugh. "Well, for starters I'm beginning to understand why life has been so confusing. I never realized how thoughts, coming from somewhere, dominate my life. But I'm just discovering I don't have to be my thoughts. This is a major breakthrough."

"And probably a relief."

"It is because I have millions of thoughts stored in my brain. And that's who I thought I was. And I'm discovering that lots of my thoughts are contradictory. So every time a thought changed, I changed. It's like the real me got lost in the confusion."

"Alan, this is an exciting discovery for you."

"Absolutely. And I'm just starting to see how important this understanding is. It feels like a wake-up call, like I'm just opening my eyes and observing the world I've created for myself. I want to ask someone, 'How did I get here?'"

Jean laughs. "That certainly seems to be the story of your life. How did you get here?"

"I'm only on the other side of the continent from my original destination," I remind her.

The sun begins to fade behind some trees and the temperature drops accordingly.

"Are you ready to go in?"

"Not quite, Jean, unless you are. I'd like to hear your feelings about this."

She leans back on the bench and breathes deeply. "If you want my honest answer, Alan, I'd say from personal experience, as well as working with clients, that you're at the proverbial fork in the road. You can either investigate who you've become by way of your thoughts or you can stay just as you are."

"I want to change."

"It's difficult," she reminds me. "Habits are like strong rubber bands. They snap you back without your realizing it."

"Nice analogy."

"It's the truth. I've seen it many times, and done it myself. We begin with good intentions but end up right where we started."

"I suppose that's because we think we want to change but don't really want to change. Hey. That could be another one of Alan's laws."

Jean smiles. "When we see how much work we have to do, we often decide that we're fine just as we are and everyone else should change instead."

"Well, I'm going to change," I insist. "And I'm going to start by trying to be aware of my Doughnut I."

She shakes her head. "Doughnut I?"

I grin and nod. "Doughnut I is the part of me that eats doughnuts when the Nondoughnut I disappears."

"Where does the Nondoughnut I go?"

"Maybe it falls asleep. My guess is that it either becomes overwhelmed with the events in life or gets bored because it can't find any meaning. I haven't worked very much with that idea."

"A good stopping place for tonight," Jean says. "I'm getting cold."

I stop, think about my body and realize I'm cold too. This leads me to another understanding. Not only don't I observe my surroundings, I'm oblivious to my physical needs as well.

We walk up to the bed and breakfast to get the room key.

"Are we Mr. and Mrs. Smith?"

"Jones."

I look surprised that she would lie.

"I'm just kidding," she assures me. "The room is in my name, two people, two beds."

"I'm paying my half," I insist.

"I know. That was our first ground rule."

The room is wonderful. And, besides that, I'm with Jean.

She asks if I have a preference for either bed.

"I suppose," I say reluctantly, "the one you're not in."

Instantly she expresses concern. "I know this was presumptuous of me and probably difficult for you. Are you sure you're all right with this?"

"Sure. I appreciate your trust and wouldn't do anything to jeopardize it."

"Thank you," she sighs.

As I head into the bathroom with my new toothbrush and pajamas she challenges, "Bet you can't brush your teeth with your left hand."

I assure her I can. A few minutes later I open the door to show her the result: toothpaste on my nose and lips. Apparently my left hand isn't proficient at brushing teeth. I'm not giving it the chance to shave me.

"Bet you can't put your left leg into your pajamas first."

"Surely that can't be difficult," I protest. With the door closed, I undress and prepare to put on the pajamas, left leg first. I lift my left leg but my right leg attempts to leave the floor at the same time. I carefully steady myself and step into the pajamas. Quite surprised, I open the door. "It's difficult."

"Like I said, habits are hard to change, especially when we're not even aware of many of them."

Realizing this could involve another discussion, Jean reaches over and turns out the light. "For tonight, that's it for me. Goodnight, Alan."

I wake up around 8:30 A.M. and have no idea where I am until I remember the bed-and-breakfast. And Jean.

Motorcycle Enlightenment

I get out of bed, look out the window and see Jean sitting beside the lake. She looks calm and peaceful. My first thought is, what can I do to help her today?

"What a nice change," a voice says. It sounds like me and may be my mind and thoughts. However, I have no idea what it intends to say. It continues: "For maybe the first time in your life, your first thought in the morning extended outward. Normally you wake up and ask what this day can do for you. How can the universe revolve around you?"

I sit still. "Was that me?"

I get up, take a quick shower, get dressed and walk out to join Jean.

"You missed half the day," she says.

"How long have you been up?"

"Since about six. I'm an early riser. I like getting up in the morning when it's quiet so I can meditate. It helps me get grounded before I meet the day's activities."

"Sounds nice. I tried meditating several years ago."

"Was it helpful?"

"I think I just sat and worried the whole time. I had read some books on how to meditate, but I couldn't do it. I gave up when I got too involved with the businesses."

"That's a shame," she says.

"Now that I've discovered the thought boxes, I see that all I did was spend time listening to and following whatever thoughts came out."

"Thought boxes?" Jean says. "You haven't mentioned them before. What about feeling boxes?"

"They're probably located in the heart and mine is padlocked."

"I hope you find the key," she says.

24.

Back at Jean's house, I make myself comfortable on the couch while she sits on the floor close by. She leans her head back and I massage her shoulders.

After a few minutes she asks, "So what about this Nondoughnut I?"

"I'm not sure," I answer. "I guess I'll read some more books."

"Just a suggestion," she adds, "but maybe the Nondoughnut I is like an inner you."

"Could be," I agree, "but how can I get inside me to find out?"

"Glad you asked. It just so happens our meditation group is meeting at my house tomorrow night. Want to come?"

"Maybe," I say cautiously, quickly previewing the situation and realizing that my Doughnut I wants to say no. Nondoughnut I is interested. "Sure," I decide. "Thanks for asking. What time?"

"Seven."

"I'll be there," I say as I stand to leave. "Thanks for a wonderful time at the bed-and-breakfast."

I start the motorcycle, wave goodbye and panic. What am I doing? I just agreed to participate in a meditation group. Am I crazy?

Motorcycle Enlightenment

From that moment until this moment I have done little but worry about the evening and whether I'll fit in and feel comfortable. But, it's six-forty-five and time to go. I ride down the street past Jean's house and see three women standing on the porch. Fear sets in and I consider riding home. But, before I can make a decision, Jean spots me. It's too late to escape.

Jean walks over as I park the cycle. "Even through the shield on your helmet I could see the fear in your eyes."

"Really? I'll have to get a darker shield."

Jean tells me they normally have five or six people, but the others were unable to attend this evening. She introduces Barbara, a massage therapist, and Lindy, a retail store owner.

"So you're Alan," Barbara states with an inquiring look.

"I am," I confess.

"It's nice to finally meet you," she says. "Jean has mentioned you frequently."

"All complimentary," Jean assures me.

I smile awkwardly, realizing that without previewing conversations I'm at a loss for words. This may be a clue as to why I'm uncomfortable in group settings.

We go inside and I sit on the couch, Jean on the chair and Barbara and Lindy on the floor. Jean begins the conversation by telling me about the group and how they get together to meditate and socialize. She asks me if I'd like to tell them about my work and why I'm here. I explain thought boxes, Doughnut I and Nondoughnut I.

Barbara suggests that Nondoughnut I might be a gestalt entity. I have no idea what she's talking about but listen attentively. Lindy offers another view. "Maybe Nondoughnut I is your inner being and by sitting in meditation you can tap into its energy and information."

I nod and begin wondering why I didn't just buy more books to read.

Barbara tells me about herself, her meditation practice and yoga. I tell her I thought yoga meant standing on your head. She stops and looks toward Lindy who picks up the conversation and talks more about the store than herself. I understand business talk and feel relaxed. I discover, though, that I've been listening too intently, tensing my neck and shoulders and causing a headache. Jean notices my situation and suggests that Barbara show me some introductory yoga exercises that might help me unwind.

"Okay," I agree, guardedly.

Barbara notices my hesitation and quickly adds, "You don't have to."

"No," I say, "I'm ready to take another step. If Jean feels this is it, it's okay with me."

Barbara gives Jean a look which I can't interpret, so I sit and worry about it.

I'm awkward and shy about doing any activity in which I'm not in control of the outcome or could be embarrassed. Audience participation terrifies me and practicing yoga in front of these women is a step too close. I don't mind looking foolish in front of others if I've planned and previewed it. But, in this situation I'm even embarrassed to take off my shoes.

Barbara does a few gentle bends and asks if I would do them too so she can get an idea of my flexibility. It's a unanimous decision that I have no flexibility. I ask Barbara if the exercises could be the wrong ones for me.

She shakes her head no. Jean pats me on the back to reassure me. Lindy asks if my muscles have always been this tight.

Motorcycle Enlightenment

"I think so," I confess.

But I keep trying. Soon I'm attempting to sit with my right heel on my left thigh while touching my right knee to the ground. Sure. My right knee barely bends and is nowhere near the floor.

Barbara encourages me. "If you do these every day for the next month, you'll see a difference. And, Alan, it would be good for you." She gives me a worksheet so I can remember the exercises. I admit I was nervous when I started but feel relaxed when I finish. Honestly I enjoyed it.

Now it's Lindy's turn. She's going to lead the meditation which is a flexibility exercise for the mind. I look at Jean and ask, "If Barbara does the yoga and Lindy the meditation, what's your duty in this threesome?"

"I serve the snacks."

I picture multi-colored sprinkled doughnuts.

"Tonight we're having amaranth crackers with royal jelly."

If I get through this evening I'm treating myself to doughnuts in the morning.

Lindy helps me with my meditation posture. She stresses maintaining a straight spine whether I sit on the floor or a chair. I try the floor but resort to a chair. They sit, it turns out, in either lotus or semi-lotus positions. I tell them if I managed it they'd have to call 911 to get me out of it.

Lindy suggests I rest my tongue against the roof of my mouth behind my front teeth. First, I realize, I have to concentrate on the fact I have a tongue which is another lesson in observation. This seems to shut off my air circulation so I put my tongue behind my bottom row of teeth. I'll work on the top later. She reminds us to breathe into the abdomen and feel the air going in and out. We may close our eyes or focus on a point just beyond our nose. I try staring at my nose but my eyes cross so I close them.

For a few minutes Lindy instructs us all to breathe calmly as she counts. She says we'll go to ten and back two times. By the count of three my mind is all over the place. I'm eating doughnuts on the boardwalk, reliving the night at the bed and breakfast, and walking on the beach. How can I have that many thoughts by the count of three? By the time Lindy gets to nine, I've relived my whole life. What can I think about on the way back to one?

Lindy stops when she gets to ten and looks at me.

"Am I in trouble?" I ask aloud.

Alan," she almost whispers, "may I give you some suggestions?"

I swallow. "Yes."

"You might find this helpful," she continues. "Imagine a line straight up and down in front of you. Try to stay focused on this line. If a thought comes up, imagine that it's pulling you either to the right or left of the line. Realize it, let the thought go and immediately return to the line. This may happen a hundred times but don't get discouraged. Just be aware of it."

"Thank you," I say, feeling guilty that everyone had to stop because of me. How did she know anyway?

We try it again. I picture the line and stay focused on it for two seconds. Then I'm riding my motorcycle with Jean, flirting with Lindy. Back to the line, I sternly tell myself. Another second on the line and I'm off. Playing tennis. Watching Bjorn Borg win Wimbledon. Playing Borg and winning. I smile, open my eyes to see if anyone is watching, and close them again. Back to the line, I say, *back!*

Even with the line, by the time we've gotten to ten

Motorcycle Enlightenment

I've ridden a hundred miles on my cycle and won a major tennis championship. Not bad for ten seconds. Then I remember that for ten seconds I was to stay focused on an imaginary straight line. Not good for ten seconds.

I know one thing for sure: I have no control over my mind. It goes and I follow. Lindy stops counting. Uh oh, in trouble now. She stopped because she had counted to ten and back twice. I missed the whole thing because I was too busy thinking about how I wasn't concentrating on counting. I slip back down on the floor to feel more like a part of the group.

"How did you do?" Lindy asks, already knowing the answer.

"Not very well," I confess. "I was all over the place. What's meditation like for you?"

"It's hard to explain," Lindy says. "After I count my breaths for a few seconds, I don't focus on anything. I can best describe it as a receptive silence. I'm not here and I'm not there. I'm present. I don't leave my body, but my mind relaxes into what I might call its natural state."

"How often do you meditate?"

"Seven days a week at five A.M."

"Why so early?"

"The morning is usually calm because the world's events haven't started."

My impression of Lindy is changing. Her quiet manner, I realize, is not a sign of shyness.

"And there's a little more to it than that," she says.

I wonder what she means but don't ask.

Lindy suggests that we all sit quietly for fifteen minutes more, a shorter time than their usual meditation. I stay on the floor and lean back against the couch. I try breathing and counting but realize I'm falling asleep when my head jerks upward. How can fifteen minutes be so long?

Finally Lindy opens her eyes and stretches her legs. The others follow.

"And now for the doughnuts?" I ask.

We eat crackers with royal jelly and talk. I decide I should leave so they can have some time together. Thanking each one I say goodnight and head for my motorcycle. The ride home is relaxing. I go inside, get ready for bed, and set my alarm for 5:00 A.M. Some part of me queries, are you sure about this? That's early. Another part of me answers, sure.

The alarm goes off at 5:00 A.M. It takes me a few minutes to reconstruct my universe and understand why there is an alarm going off beside my bed. It is a quieter world at this time of day, I remind myself. The part of me that wants to sleep says, of course it's quiet. Every sane person is still asleep.

I go downstairs where it's less tempting to crawl back into bed. First my yoga exercises. I sit down on the floor and feel a heavy hand pushing me back. Go back to sleep right here on the living room floor, it advises. I resist and begin the exercises. In a few minutes I feel better. I can feel something tingling through my body. The exercises take twenty minutes and I feel refreshed. I stand up, stretch and walk around a little.

Next is meditation. I use the straight-back desk chair. I mentally draw the line in front of me and begin counting my breaths. One, and I'm off. How in the world is that possible? I can't concentrate even for one second. I remind myself that Lindy said not to get upset so I relax and try again. I sort of get to three. I try stringing the numbers together in my mind so I won't lose the continuity, but my thoughts are too strong. I try for about fifteen minutes but never get to ten. Each time I lose control, I start over at one because I can't remember where I was when I lost count. I think about the thought boxes. Mine are packed.

After twenty minutes I give up and reward myself by going back to bed for another hour. An hour turns into more until the telephone rings and wakes me up.

"How did it go?" Jean asks.

"Shaky," I admit.

"You sound sleepy."

"I got up for the first time at five," I proudly admit.

"It's nine now," she says. "Time to get up for the second time."

25.

I think about getting up but don't want to. I'm a little discouraged because it's difficult to admit that Doughnut I is in control of my life. My perceptions and memories of the past have become my habits which have become me. I wonder what would happen if I suddenly became Nondoughnut I. Would all my questions about the universe be answered? And, if they were, what would I do?

I force myself out of bed, shower, eat and sit down with my stack of three-by-five cards. I discover that today is wash day. This is a chore, I tell myself. If I were enlightened I wouldn't have to do this. I trudge out the door with my laundry bag and detergent.

Mrs. Crawley is watering her flowers.

"Good morning, Alan. Off to do the wash?"

"Yeah," I answer unhappily.

"I can tell by the sound of your voice it's not something you enjoy. I love doing the wash."

I almost ask her to do mine. "Well, I don't like it, but it has to be done," I answer.

"Make the best of it," she says cheerily.

As I walk I think. Who is it who doesn't like to do the wash? Who can't focus during meditation? Who doesn't want to get up at five? What does being enlightened mean? Where would I go if I were enlightened? Lost in a maze of thoughts, I mechanically head down the street.

I enter the laundromat and say hello to a woman and young girl, presumably her daughter. As I begin tossing my wash into a machine, I glance up and see the woman wince as I put my green dishcloth in with my white underwear.

The washer stops. I unload it by throwing the laundry across the room into the dryer. The young girl admires my aim. Her mother carefully shakes each piece of their laundry and puts it into the dryer. My sleep socks, the ones with the holes in them, miss the dryer and land on the floor. The young girl runs over, picks them up, laughs, and holds them up to show her mother. They aren't really socks anymore because the heels and toes are completely gone and all that's left is the part that covers the top and bottom of my foot and ankle. Her mother shakes her head and tells her daughter to throw them into the dryer. I insert my quarters, push the "dry" button and sit down to wait.

It occurs to me, that even if I were enlightened, I would still have to sit here and wait for my wash to dry. So what's the point of becoming enlightened or having my questions answered by the universe? I'll still have to get up in the morning and eat breakfast. The world is not going to change. I've never thought about this before. If a fairy with a magic wand suddenly appeared and granted all my wishes, what would I do? If I knew who I was, what the purpose of life was, and everything else, what would change?

These questions occupy me until the dryer stops. I

take the laundry out and stuff it into a bag. Mother and daughter are folding theirs. I smile at them and leave.

I walk and think some more. This is major, I tell myself. How could I have missed this question before? What will I do when I find the answers? I guess it depends on the answers I get. That soothes me for awhile. A quotation from the *Tao Te Ching* pops into my mind: "Fish must not leave the stream." I never gave that much thought before. Even if a fish becomes enlightened, he'd still have to swim in the water. He probably wouldn't stand up and walk upstream. I'll probably live here on earth until I die, enlightened or not.

I take my laundry into the living room, think about the mother and her daughter and decide to fold my clothes. Maybe the dishcloth should have been washed separately from my underwear. Soon the chore I procrastinated doing is over and it wasn't so bad.

26.

It's been days since I sat on the boardwalk benches. Sitting beside the ocean is the closest I've been to meditating. To me, the experience is similar to the way Lindy described her meditation. I walk up on the boardwalk and over to the benches. I don't recognize anyone. There's a new cast of characters. Vacation groups must have changed.

My favorite bench is vacant, so I sit down facing the water and feel uplifted immediately. I decide to listen not only to the ocean but to observe what's going on inside my mind. In a few minutes a jigsaw puzzle appears in the sky in front of me. It's so vivid I wonder if the people sitting around me can see it too. The puzzle would be complete except for a few empty spaces. It's obvious that it's been forced together. I smile and think to myself, that puzzle looks like something I put together. If something doesn't fit, make it. Another of Alan's laws.

Suddenly a pleasant, soothing voice speaks to me. It says something like this: "You've tried to force the puzzle of life together to make it fit your expectations. But now it's time to see that the end result is not as important as the process. Let each piece appear when it does, then consciously work with it."

"Okay," I answer the voice. I realize where I am and pretend to clear my throat. That way if I had actually said "okay" aloud, people might think that I was only coughing.

I breathe deeply and want to return to that moment. How can I describe it? A religious phrase comes to mind, "The peace of God that passeth all understanding." With that voice was a calmness, a serenity beyond this world. It was wonderful. It lasted thirty seconds.

I'm tempted to ask the person next to me if he saw a large puzzle in the sky and heard a voice. I decide against this.

I pull out my notebook and write down the message. All I can think about is returning to that moment when I felt so peaceful. Next a thought comes that feels like a graceful opening, like a flower unfolding its petals. Instead of frustrating myself trying to make the Earth and its events suit me, I can change how I perceive and respond to them. I've read this information in a hundred books. But until I experienced that inner peace for myself, no matter how briefly, I didn't really understand. Now I know it's possible.

As I continue sitting on the bench, I experience a second opening. For an instant I know all I want to know. It is like looking at a thousand page novel, and in one second, knowing, seeing and living everything in it.

Instead of relaxing into the experience, I grab my notebook and start writing. If I could remember everything I'm feeling this instant, the book and my life would be complete. But at the thought of writing it down, it disappears. The event lasted no more than fifteen seconds.

Again I try to regain the moment. I sit exactly as I was sitting. I stare at exactly the same spot on the ocean.

Motorcycle Enlightenment

I breathe deeply. I count my breaths. I close my eyes. I do everything but re-experience the moment. "Darn," I say, apparently out loud because the man next to me says, "Pardon?"

"Sorry," I answer. "I was talking to myself."

He gives me a look and glances at the woman next to him. In their silent communication they ask one another if they should go. They stay and I leave.

Walking along the boardwalk, I realize what just happened. I experienced an inner peace and merged momentarily with my inner being. "Goodness," I start to say aloud but catch myself before anyone hears me.

27.

Back at the apartment I take a nap and then call Jean to tell her about my experience, but she's with a client. She doesn't have time to talk and is busy tonight. I tell her I understand and don't mention the purpose of my call.

I know, somehow, that this peaceful feeling is related to my search and the meaning of life. I walk to Lindy's store, but she isn't there. Guess I'm not supposed to tell anyone.

It's now dinner time so I eat because I don't know what else to do. In fact, I have no desire to do anything but return to that earlier moment. I feel like a fish looking for the stream, knowing that I'm already here in the stream.

After dinner I walk around the house. All I can see is a block of time between now and going to bed, but I don't know how to fill it. Somewhere mid-step between the living room and the kitchen, this thought occurs to me: Doughnut I doesn't know what to do. It's not used to being watched.

I go to the computer, open a file called "Doughnut" and write: "From the moment of birth I begin developing a 'self' which learns how to cope with the world. This self is my ego or personality. It's the mechanism that learns how to deal with life. It knows that I seek happiness and try to avoid suffering. Therefore, its job is to be vigilant and find only situations that meet my expectations."

But another part of me has awakened—Nondoughnut I—the part that was shocked the moment it realized that a doughnut had been eaten without its awareness.

So here I am caught between the two parts of me. I visualize a colt trying to stand on his legs for the first time. I need strength but I also need a reason for standing.

I conceive a story about a boy who wants to be a knight. He crawls into an adult's suit of armor, but being young, he can't move and gets stuck. Eventually he falls asleep, and sleeps for years. One day he's hit with a sword which awakens him. He's shocked to find out that somehow he has grown up inside the armor and lived as a knight, but not the one of his earlier dreams. Slowly he disassociates from all he has become and changes his ways. By the end of his life he is the real knight he had envisioned himself to be.

I am very much like that boy. Only I feel like three different Alans. Doughnut I or Alan 1 is the present-day knight; Nondoughnut I or Alan 2 is the boy waking up; The "I" observing this, Alan 3, may be the knight I wish to become.

It's late and we Alans are heading for bed.

28.

At 5:00 A.M. the alarm goes off. I wake up, go downstairs, practice yoga, and sit on the chair to meditate. I count breaths, soon forget them, and think about Jean. I'm sitting on the chair, eyes closed, watching images of us at the bed-and-breakfast. Sometimes I smile and almost laugh. Meditation comes to an end and I look at the clock. Twenty minutes.

Wasn't that a pleasant meditation? I say to myself. Another part of me answers, maybe not. Instead of getting up I sit longer to contemplate this matter.

I breathe deeply and let the question roll around by itself for awhile as I wait for an answer. Slowly it comes.

The time was spent following thoughts as they flowed out of the thought boxes; therefore, the ego or the personality was in control. The idea, of course, is to allow the logical, thinking mind to rest so that information can flow from the inner being.

I sit for another twenty minutes. I observe lots of thoughts that move through, but I keep the breath counting foremost in my mind. I make it to ten and back *twice*! Thoughts are now like an undercurrent. They flow, but I don't stop to focus on them. Thoughts must be a

Motorcycle Enlightenment

constant of the mind until the thought boxes are emptied. Can the thought boxes be emptied?

I finish, move my limbs, and stand up. I get the weirdest feeling I ever felt in my life. It's as if I've stepped into an abyss. Here I have a whole day before me, and I just finished all that I intend to do. It's seven A.M. I sit down to catch my breath. I see what could be a danger. My intention is to examine Doughnut I or Alan 1's habits and patterns and discover who I have become. In the process I'm going to explore my constricting perceptions of both me and the world and let them go. But what happens to me, Alan 1? It's like pulling the rug out from under my feet only to realize there is no floor.

I imagine the process of self-observation is long and slow. I have lots of thoughts and habits packed into the thought boxes. Trying to observe and change them is like trying to dismantle who I think I am. I have become my habits and patterns. I react to every stimulus in the world this way. Now I think I'm ready to dismiss the ego and thank it for observing, filing, processing, and responding to everything for all these years because I don't need it any longer.

The ego retorts, "Yeah, sure. I've heard all that before. You'll come running back as soon as you experience suffering. I know you."

I think it has a point.

29.

The telephone rings, startling me.

"Are you busy?" Jean asks.

"No."

"Would you like some company?"

"Of course. How soon?"

"Ten minutes."

About twenty minutes later Jean knocks on the door.

When I answer she skips hello and says, "May I read your book?"

"The book? It's not finished."

"I have the day off."

I stand there considering. If it isn't any good, I'll be embarrassed. But I think it's okay. It may not be for anyone else, but it's been therapy for me. Somehow I thought I would find the answers to my questions then write the book. I didn't know that writing the book itself would be the answer.

"Where is it?" Jean asks.

"In the computer. I had pictured us sitting on the lifeguard chair the first time you read it."

"I don't think they share them during the day."

"Okay," I relent. "But I'd like to watch."

"Watch me read?"

"Yes. And tell me everything you like and don't like. Deal?"

"We'll see," she says cautiously.

I sit down at the computer and open the file. I'm nervous. When everything's ready I move aside and Jean sits in front of the screen.

"Don't read too fast, okay?"

"You're really going to watch me read?"

"Yes."

I stand beside her and watch each expression intently. When she smiles, I smile. When she frowns, I frown. Soon I'm sitting beside her reading every word. When she pauses, I ask what's wrong. We intersperse bathroom and snack breaks with reading until we finish the rough draft. I wait for her final comments. There are none. Jean leans back in her chair.

Why doesn't she say she loves the book? Or that she hates it? Why doesn't she say anything?

"Let's go for a walk on the beach," she suggests.

Confused, I agree.

We walk and hold hands. It's nice but I'm tense. What is she thinking, or feeling?

Finally she says, "Alan, you're too attached to the book. If I say it's good, you'll be elated. If I say it needs work, you'll be crushed. Right?"

"Of course," I admit.

"But, who's elated and who's crushed?"

I don't answer. "This isn't exactly how I pictured the day you would finally read the book," I respond.

"Isn't it Alan 1 who is so interested in my opinion?"

I want to sulk and walk away but I know she's right. "This is bitter medicine," I tell her.

"It's not medicine at all."

"You've just read the result of years of reading, and living," I persist.

"That's precisely the point. You see the book as Alan 1's accomplishment which you want to be finished and perfect." She pauses and asks, "May I call Alan 1 the outer self and Alan 2 the inner self?"

"Sure," I say, not caring whether she calls them Alan or Harry.

"It's your path" she says. "Maybe for now you can see this book as the path you've followed. Call it your 'Where I've Been and Where I Am' journal. Maybe it's your journey. It's constantly changing."

"Hmmm," I respond.

She looks at me and waits for the light to go on in my head.

I look at her and wait for more information.

"Hmmm," I verbalize again, indicating a malfunctioning light.

"So," she continues. "It's not my path, and it might not be the next person's either. That's not important. What is important is that you're beginning to realize who you are. It's not about whether I like the words on the page or not."

We walk several blocks, still hand in hand, but quiet. "So where do you think the book will take you?"

"Where?" I repeat, still waiting for her to say she loves the book.

She knows I'm disappointed but her look encourages me.

Suddenly I think I see where's she going with this question. "I get it! I thought the book was going to be my story of enlightenment as I rode from the East coast to the West coast. But, it's an inner journey, a kind of motorcycle enlightenment. Why, that's great. I'm glad I thought of it," I tease.

"I'm glad you did too," she smiles. "And wouldn't it be interesting," she adds, "if along the road you meet three Alans that all turn out to be you?"

"Sure," I agree.

Jean smiles endearingly. I know she's just done what I was unable to do myself. She has helped me change my thoughts and feelings. Hopefully, someday, I'll learn to do it myself. I know I'm off again but I have no idea where the next road begins.

After a few minutes I begin to ramble. "Do you know what I think?"

She bursts out laughing and I join her. "You always do this to me," I tell her. "It's not my fault. I'm just walking along, minding my own business, feeling peaceful and calm, and you act as a catalyst for a thought box."

"Guilty," she admits. "So what are you thinking this time?"

"Well," I begin, "I think the three Alans each view the world from a different perspective. Alan 1 is the mechanical me that reacts to events in the world based on his previous experiences. Alan 2 sees himself and Alan 1 from an inner or higher perspective. He sees everything in its interconnected form and gives me insights to help me grow and expand. I think you saw his eyes from the very beginning."

"That's interesting. And what about Alan 3?"

"I think I have to experience Alan 2 first. What do you think?"

"Maybe." Then she says, "I like the book."

I'm glad and relieved.

Jean begins to say something, hesitates, and starts again.

"I was concerned."

"About what?"

"That your interest in changing was just so you had material for your book and that you would give up when you finished writing. But you seem quite serious about continuing."

"I am," I assure her.

We walk farther along the beach. I notice that Jean seems rather pensive. "What are you thinking?" I ask.

"I was just remembering Stuart Crawley, how much he would have enjoyed your book. He would have been pleased with the effort you're making. I was fortunate to have his help. Without him I don't know where I'd be today."

"Really? I can't picture you struggling with life."

"I did." She shakes her head. "When I was a therapist I was advising people how to live their lives while my own was in disarray. After the divorce I fell apart. The Crawleys were so helpful. With their guidance I began looking at who I really was and not who I imagined myself to be. That took a lot of work. Eventually I knew who I wanted to become."

"That's where I am now. I don't know what I want to do with my life."

"That's not what I mean," Jean says. "I decided on the person I wanted to be no matter what happened in my life. I was more interested in being than doing."

This isn't clear to me. "I thought life was all about doing. I've always tried 'doing' the right thing so I could be perfect and then, hopefully, disappear. I never thought about just being."

Jean frowns. "When you say that it worries me. I'm not certain I want to get more involved with a person whose goal is not to be here."

"I hadn't thought about that," I admit. "I suppose it doesn't encourage a long-term relationship if I'm planning to disappear."

30.

We walk to Jean's house because it's closer, even though her car's at my place. Jean prepares dinner and we eat, mostly in silence

"Would you turn off the thought factory for a minute?" she asks.

I make a sound as if machines are grinding to a halt.

"What are you thinking about now?"

"Being."

"You can't figure that out. It short circuits the brain. It's like the question about a tree falling in the woods. Does it make a sound if no one is there? The analytical mind will dissect and analyze it based on the definitions of sound and hearing. Textbooks can be written about it. Or about what is the sound of one hand clapping?"

"How does one hand clap?" I ask.

She rolls her eyes.

"Did I miss the point?"

"There is no point. That's the point."

"That sounds like a riddle world."

"That's a good analogy."

"I was kidding."

Motorcycle Enlightenment

We straighten up the kitchen and sit down in the living room. "You know," Jean says, "my car is over at your place, and you look too tired to walk home. But Alice will think I stayed at your house all night."

"She'll be extremely pleased. In fact, I think I'll tell her you did stay just to make her happy."

Jean ignores my comment and suggests, "Why don't you stay here and we'll get up early tomorrow morning and walk over?"

"I like everything except the getting up early. Do you mean before five?"

"No," she assures me. "You can do your yoga and meditation here. Then we'll go. You don't have to change your routine."

"I could, but I'd rather not."

"I know. Yoga and meditation are at five. Not five-forty-five and certainly not at six. You get attached to the time. This is when you do yoga and meditation. At seven they're over. Then if you're not working on your book, you wonder what to do the rest of the day?"

"How do you know that?" I ask.

"Because I'm getting to know you better."

"So you're saying that doing yoga and meditation at five is wrong?"

"No."

"I don't understand."

Jean starts singing, "The wheels on the bus go round and round."

I look at her and say, "Of course there's no point, but what's the point?"

"You're like walking Velcro," she says. "You grasp and attach to everything because, for you, everything has to have its definite purpose. You do this *now*. You do that *later.* Each part of your life is segmented and separated. *This* is the time to eat. *This* is the time to read. *This* to meditate. *This* to see Jean. *This* to be alone."

"The point being?"

"You drive yourself crazy. I'll bet when you owned your businesses, you had a definite time to work. When work was over, you had time to relax. Work and relax were opposites."

"Yes they were. And if I had to attend to business matters when I should have been relaxing, it ruined my mood and probably everyone else's who had to be around me. No kidding."

"I know you're not kidding," Jean says. "It's the result of trying and doing. It's living life as if it's an end in itself in which each activity has to be done in a particular way to produce a certain result. If it does you're happy. If it doesn't you're unhappy. You divide life into segments. You have one category for self, one for others, one for time, one for space, one for here, one for there, one for now, one for later, one for work, one for relaxation, one for Jean, one for Alan, one for . . ."

"I get the point," I say.

"You have so many walls and barriers, you're suffocating yourself. When you dissolve one, you think you've dissolved them all. And your mind deludes you into thinking you did. You're elated. Everything is fine. But soon, that creeping, gnawing dissatisfaction sets in and you feel empty. The world seems pointless. You can't find meaning. You get depressed. You want to do something. Am I getting warm?"

"Hot!" I exclaim. "But what do I do?"

Jean conceals a smile.

I answer myself. "I don't do anything. I be. When I

stop trying to do, I automatically am." I sit and "be" which lasts a few seconds. "I'm stuck," I confess.

"You're not stuck," Jean says. "But maybe the 'thinking-doing' part of you is."

"No, I'm stuck," I repeat.

She gently places her hand on my arm. "Maybe that's enough for today. 'Being' can't be forced. It's a natural state. A knowing or feeling of wholeness. A connection with everything."

That stirs something within me, like a memory I'd forgotten long ago. "That's comforting, Jean. I like that."

"Good. I'm certain you can relate to it. It's those times when you feel energy flowing and you know, intuitively, that you are that energy."

"Ah, like the energy at the lighthouse," I recall. "Like I'm moving and not moving. I see how this could work." It feels as if a log jam has been broken up. "This *is* interesting. So I'm energy and, when I'm in touch with it and allowing it to flow naturally, I'm being. But when I try to direct it and force it the way I want it to flow, I'm doing."

"Okay," Jean agrees.

I continue. "If this is right, then it's a crucial understanding. It would explain who I am. I'm energy but I'm also Alan. And Alan is the personality that I've formed based on my past experiences, the mechanical portion of me which perpetuates automatic doing. Isn't this fascinating?"

Jean smiles at my enthusiasm.

"And energy is another word for essence. Yes. Of course. I've read about essence. And therefore everything is essence. It just is. Understanding this is being. So, what I have to do is observe myself and undo who

I've become so I can return to who I am—essence. This makes sense."

"Good," Jean says. "That's what Stuart helped me to understand. We're essence experiencing ourselves. But we get confused and think that we have to do things in order to become who we already are."

"Right. So we're all essence and therefore all connected. Why is that so difficult to accept? I wonder why we're all essence in different forms. I mean, if you're essence and I'm essence and the table is essence, what makes you, you, and me, me, and the table a table?"

"I don't know," she replies a little wearily.

"Well, we can't stop here. We have to figure this out," I insist.

"Maybe those answers will come to you when you're ready. But I doubt if sitting here using your finite, intellectual mind to fathom the infinite will work."

"Using the finite, intellectual mind to fathom the infinite," I repeat. "That's intriguing. So how do we comprehend the infinite?"

Jean's eyes roll and she reaches toward the bookcase and pulls out a book. My eyes open wide. I think she has *the* book where all of this is explained.

"Nope," she says, "isn't there."

"What's not there?" I ask impatiently.

She hands me the book. It's a dictionary.

"I was looking for your photo under the word 'analytical,' but it's not there."

I hand her the book. "That bad?"

"You just never give up. You know that jigsaw puzzle you mentioned?"

"Yes."

"With your analytical mind, you're always creating

more pieces that have to be forced together. Today the puzzle has a hundred. Tomorrow a thousand."

"What do you mean?"

"The more you analyze everything, the more pieces you *create*. You're searching desperately for the truth but you run right past it. Apparently you want it to be more grandiose."

"I suppose I'm 'doing' again."

"It needs to be a balance, a combination of the head and the heart. Being is like opening your heart."

"Surgically?"

She half-smiles. "You struggle so hard. It doesn't have to be difficult. Stop trying and doing. *Be*."

"I'll try," I say, hearing my own words and wanting to change them. I don't know how to respond. Maybe silence is the answer.

Eventually Jean takes a break which encourages me to get up and do the same. A short while later we're both back on the couch. I stretch out and gently pull her towards me so that we're both reclining. She's in my arms and soon we're asleep. At some point in the night I wake up, have no idea where I am, but feel Jean beside me. I sigh with contentment and go back to sleep. A few hours later Jean stirs and wakes me again. I peek at my watch and try not to disturb her. It's five A.M. Slipping carefully onto the floor, I sit in my semi-semi lotus position. Instead of concentrating on counting, I hear my mind say: open your heart.

My thoughts are scattered as usual. What about this relationship? How can I be and do? What are these walls and barriers? How do I fathom the infinite?

Jeans rolls over and taps me on the shoulder. "Your thinking woke me up," she says.

"How can my thinking wake you up?"

"Energy," she says, "All thoughts are energy. If we hooked you up to a generator, you'd power North America."

31.

Jean tries to sleep longer but can't. She gets up, goes upstairs and does her meditation before preparing for work. I do yoga. Since I did meditation before yoga, I worry if this will have an adverse affect on my day. I almost wait to hear Jean call out from the bathroom, "It won't." She doesn't so I hope my day will be alright.

We walk to my apartment but not as early as we had planned. Mrs. Crawley surely sees us, but we don't see her. She must be wondering why Jean's car was here and we were somewhere else.

After saying goodbye to Jean, my next thought is about sleeping. My second and third thoughts are the same so I sleep. About nine-thirty I wake up and start my day for the second time. I decide a stroll on the beach is just what I need. I walk out the front door and see Mrs. Crawley.

"Good morning," she says, pauses and hopes I'll answer the question she doesn't ask.

"Good morning," I say and don't answer her unasked question. "Trimming?" I say instead.

"Oh, yes," she replies. "Sometimes it gets to be too much for me, but I love being in the sun and working in the yard."

"I see," I say, not seeing at all. "You like this?" I ask again.

She puts down the trimmers and looks up. "Don't you like yard work?"

"It's not my favorite," I tell her. "I had to mow the grass when I was a kid. After I was married, Sheila and the kids did it. After I got divorced, I lived in an apartment."

"That's a shame."

"Why?" I wonder aloud.

"Because everyone needs to touch the earth now and then."

I smile at her answer, bend down and pat the ground. "That should do it for about a week."

Mystified, she asks, "What *do* you like?" She hesitates and adds, "If you don't mind my asking."

I sigh and sit down beside her on the grass. "I don't know, Mrs. Crawley. I honestly don't know. There aren't many things I like."

"I thought that might be the case."

"Are you sure you and Jean aren't related?" I ask, half kidding.

"No," she laughs. "I can just tell things about you."

I'm waiting for her to refer to my eyes but she says, "By the way you walk."

This surprises me. "How so?"

"Oh, you can tell a lot about a person by the way they carry themselves. Jean, for instance, is spontaneous and loving. People know she genuinely cares about them. But I've watched how you stay to yourself. Don't get me wrong. You're polite and kind, very courteous, but there's another you inside. Do you know what I mean?"

"Unfortunately, I do." I tell her. "It's like there are walls between me and everyone else."

"Exactly," she says. "When I talk to you, I don't feel as if I'm talking to you. I can't really explain any more. It's an odd sensation. I shouldn't tell you this. It'll embarrass you."

"No, Mrs. Crawley, you're precisely right."

She goes back to trimming. While I'm sitting beside her, I reach over and pull a weed out of the flower bed. A few minutes later I pull another one.

While continuing to find weeds and extract them I say, "Jean told me about Mr. Crawley. He must have been an interesting person. What was he like?"

"A real and gentle man." she explains. "He was always reading and writing, a lot like you. Somehow he had a different perspective on life. He always looked for the good and made everyone feel special."

"Jean seems to have thought a great deal of him."

"Yes. Stuart helped her through some hard times, especially when she and Edward divorced. But," she stops herself, "that's for Jean to tell you, not me."

"She told me a little already," I say, hoping she'll add more details.

She doesn't, at first.

I stare at Mrs. Crawley, the sun making her white hair shine, as she snips here and there. She looks like the personification of joy.

"I'm very fond of Jean," I confess, "but . . . I don't know," not finishing the thought.

"Just be patient," she advises. "Like these flowers, everything blooms at the right time." Changing the subject she says, "I've been thinking lately and wondering if you would help me."

"Help you? How in the world could I help you?"

"Well," she begins, "Stuart and I were working on

an idea just before he died. Actually Jean was the inspiration for it when her life turned upside down. She spent days at our house because she didn't want to be alone. That gave the three of us plenty of time to sit and talk for hours. We realized that there were lots of people in the same situation as Jean who needed a place to put themselves back together."

"I would have been one too," I add.

She continues, "We had begun taking steps to make this idea into a reality, but with Stuart's death plans came to a halt. I would still like it to come true, but I don't have the necessary business knowledge. Apparently you do."

"Well, I can certainly handle the accounting and the behind-the-scenes organization. Just let me know."

We continue moving around the yard, weeding and talking. Mrs. Crawley asks more questions about my life and I answer, probably in too much detail. But she seems interested. Soon, most of the weeds are gone. In the process I discover that the boundary between the activity and me dissolved, just as when I'm riding my bicycle on the boardwalk or watching the ocean.

Mrs. Crawley was obviously aware of the situation but didn't point it out. She just kept asking and working. And I kept talking, without previewing or postviewing my thoughts. Maybe I was being and doing yard work.

Mrs. Crawley stands up, looks over her meticulously weeded garden and thanks me.

The funny thing is I was here and pulling weeds. If I had known last night that I had to help Mrs. Crawley work in her yard, it would have ruined everything. All I would have focused on was how much I objected to yard work and pulling weeds.

"Would you like to have lunch with me?" Mrs. Crawley asks.

"That would be nice. Thank you."

Now I think about it. Why did I say yes? I'm nervous. Suppose I don't like what she's making? Will this take all afternoon? Now I can't walk on the beach. I won't have time to meditate on how to "be." Where do these thoughts come from? Better yet, how do I stop them?

Mrs. Crawley prepares a delicious lunch. We eat and reminisce about the old days in Ocean City, and she tells me more about her life with Mr. Crawley and about their idea for a center where people could be together and help one another.

"Do you really think this concept is possible?" The business aspect of my mind is interested in being active again.

"More so than ever," she responds. "There's a property for sale just south of Ocean City that would be ideal. It has two large houses sitting on the beach. I called and inquired about them, but dealing with the finances and getting it started is too much for me."

"I would be glad to help."

"Thank you, Alan. I need to do some more thinking and I want to see if Jean's ready too."

"Jean?" I say, wondering how she fits into the picture.

"Oh, yes. Jean's an essential part. She's an excellent therapist and I wouldn't do this without her. I know she likes working in the real estate office but I believe her heart is in counseling."

"I think Jean wants to be my therapist. Maybe she believes there's hope for me."

Mrs. Crawley laughs. "I'm sure there's hope for you,

Alan. And I'm sure that Jean likes you a lot. We have many telephone conversations when she's not with you."

I take a deep breath and slowly exhale. "Well, in any case, Jean has helped me and I'm very fond of her. I'll follow your advice and try being patient. It will be a new experience."

After lunch Mrs. Crawley excuses herself from the table, goes upstairs and returns with a photo of Mr. Crawley.

Just looking at him makes me smile. "He looks like a person who enjoyed life," I comment.

"Yes, he did. He was content wherever he was. That's what made him unique. It was like he saw the world from a different perspective."

"What do you mean?"

"Oh, let's see," she says. "He always had new 'theories' as he called them. One of my favorites was his idea of 'I Am That' or 'I Am Not That.' He believed in the goodness of all beings and knew that we are all connected. In every situation he said we have a choice to be connected and loving which is 'I Am That' or disconnected and fearful which is 'I Am Not That.' He made it so simple. After he had this insight, I could almost see his internal process at work as he explored the options in every situation and chose 'I Am That.' Eventually it became who he was. You might say he was very consistent."

"I wish I could have met him."

"You would have liked him, and I'm certain he would have liked you too."

Before we know it, half the afternoon is gone. Mrs. Crawley looks at the clock. "Oh, I'm sorry, Alan, I've kept you all day. You certainly didn't want to spend your whole day talking to me."

Motorcycle Enlightenment

"Mrs. Crawley, talking with you is wonderful. I enjoy every minute of it."

"You run along," she tells me. "I'll clean up."

Instead of heading for the beach I return to my apartment and type a file called "I Am That." I finish and sit down on the couch to reflect on the day's events. I thought I would spend the day on the boardwalk and instead I weeded the garden and had lunch with Mrs. Crawley. In retrospect I enjoyed both very much. But, if I had previewed these activities, I wouldn't have done them.

I think I'm on to something concerning "be" and "do" and how they can be the same thing. If I know about an event in advance, I analyze, dissect and ruin it. I take all the available data, funnel it through my perceptions, the walls and barriers, determine how I expect it to unfold, and frustrate myself trying to make it conform. But if I can relax wherever I am and "be," then I can flow with the energy and "do."

32.

The next morning I'm up at five and do yoga and meditation. Still sitting on the floor I begin to ponder.

I suppose the walls and barriers that separate me from me, and me from others are the same ones that separate be and do. To remove the walls means contemplating who I think I am and how I project myself in the world. All of this, I presume, is predicated on the beliefs that have been filed by the ego. But what are those deeply held beliefs? Where do I start looking for them? This could take a lot of work. Suddenly I say, "Ahhhh" and I know this is audible. I wonder if this is what the voice meant when it said a "journey of great proportions." This is even farther than California.

Remembering that voice in the night makes me wonder if dreams are somehow connected to the walls and barriers. Maybe when I sleep, part of me stays awake and converses with Alan 2 or 3. Maybe they use symbols to help me understand. And maybe that's why I like to sleep so much. It sounds like a perfect excuse to me.

As I sit and let my mind wander, I feel a presence. Without words it communicates information. I sense all creation emanating from an Unnamable Essence, an energy beyond even the most far-reaching thoughts of the finite mind. I know unmistakably that I am this essence. I see an image of flowers unfolding within flowers within flowers. The scene appears to be endless.

Another image comes of thousands of robots walking around in a city. I know I'm one of them although they all look the same. The metal covering of the robots represents walls and barriers. I sense it is a fearful and greedy place where the robots believe they have to "take" from others before they are "taken from." They are always on guard and protective. Life is obviously very mechanical and has no meaning.

The presence explains that this image represents our present state of life on Earth. We have identified ourselves with this robotic view of a separate self and become attached to the world of senses. Intuitively we know our essence but have forgotten. We immerse ourselves in activities in order to mask the emptiness. Eventually we believe our external search for happiness is the only purpose for our being on Earth. We forget that we are here to evolve through joyful, loving experiences.

Our inner being is always aware of our situation but cannot interfere without our request for assistance. Nudges, hints, seeming coincidences, even strange feelings, are the methods by which the inner being stays in touch. We sense these and know which choices will bring us the most contentment and joy. But often we choose otherwise because of our fears and distorted beliefs.

The images and the voices stop. I look around the room and orient myself. It seems as if days have passed, but I look at the clock and see that only a few hours have elapsed. I stand up, stretch and head for the kitchen. Just then the phone rings. It occurs to me that had the phone rung five minutes earlier it would have startled me.

Interesting timing. It's probably Jean. But then she's the only one who ever calls.

I pick up the phone and say, "Hello, Jean."

"Hello, Alan," she responds and adds, "But isn't that backwards? Aren't I supposed to tell you who's calling?"

"I just knew it was you. You're timing's perfect," I assure her.

"Are you being?" she asks, maybe jokingly.

"Call it meditating," I respond.

"Sorry to disturb you."

"It's okay."

"Want to go out for dinner?"

My first thought is no. I want to go back into that state and learn more, but I stop myself and say, "Sure, what time?"

"Six," she says.

"Ish," I correct.

33.

I sit down and try to recapture the mood. It's gone. I look at the clock and see that it's only eight-thirty which makes for a long day. I think about getting ready since "ish" can sometimes mean before six. But I stop. "Alan," I say, "you can't get ready for dinner at eight-thirty in the morning and sit and wait all day."

I eat breakfast, slowly. I take a long, long walk, slowly. I nap. I look at the clock about a hundred times. The day passes uneventfully. Finally, Jean arrives.

I greet her at the door and tell her she looks stunning.

There's an awkward silence. Something isn't right. "So, where are we going for dinner?" I ask.

"Your choice," Jean replies.

"Let's eat on the boardwalk and sit on the lifeguard's chair when it's dark."

"Okay," she shrugs. "That's fine with me."

We stroll slowly over to the boardwalk as I tell her about weeding the garden and having lunch with Mrs. Crawley. She pretends to swoon.

"What's come over you?"

"I have this good friend who's helping me," I answer. "She says things that completely unnerve me and later I find out she's right. She's amazing."

"I hope to meet her someday." Jean softens.

"You will," I assure her. "And I'm sure you'll like her."

After dinner we head for the far end of the boardwalk. Soon it's dark. We take off our shoes and socks, head out onto the beach, and climb the lifeguard's chair. Hours seemingly go by as we watch the ocean. It doesn't go anywhere. We talk a little. I don't process my thoughts aloud. She doesn't ask any questions.

I think I could fall in love this minute. Part of me wants to tell Jean I think I love her. Part of me has no idea what relationships are all about.

Maybe it's just the outer self, that sense-seeking Alan 1 looking for pleasure, I remind myself. And maybe I still think Jean's the perfect ice cream cone. I don't know. My thoughts run in circles.

I look at the ocean and try to focus on the waves. If she can read my mind, I want it to be on the water in front of me. Not on what I was thinking.

"What are you thinking now?" she pries.

"How calm the ocean looks," I lie.

She touches my nose.

"What are you doing?"

"Checking to see if it's growing," she teases.

"You're good."

She sits forward. "Your breath is short and shallow which means your brain is in high gear. Any confessions?" she tries again.

"Oh, Jean, I don't know. I was thinking that I'd like to say I love you but I can't. I don't want to ruin what we have by forcing more, but sometimes it gets confusing."

"I'm sorry, Alan. I don't want to complicate your life." She leans back and stares into the darkness.

Motorcycle Enlightenment

Minutes go by. Her breathing is short and shallow, a rarity. "Alan," she finally begins. "I really am sorry. I like you, but part of me is scared."

"Of me?" I interject, somehow hurt.

"A little," she agrees and clarifies. "Sometimes I just feel that you believe I'm the missing piece in your life, but I'm not."

She pauses. I wait for more.

"I guess I thought Edward would make my life perfect. Maybe for you it was your businesses and family. I don't know. The Crawleys helped me start over. I learned to accept who I am—to be—and from there I was able to do things again. But I guess I've kept one big wall in place to prevent me from getting hurt again."

"I won't hurt you, Jean," I whisper in her ear.

"Not intentionally, I know you won't. But . . ."

"But I'm still neurotic," I say, finishing her sentence. "You don't have to tell me. I live with me."

She forces a smile. "What shall we do, Alan?"

"Mrs. Crawley told me about her idea to purchase property and start a center. Maybe we could help her."

"We could, but right now that would be avoiding the issue. What about us?"

"Jean, I live in my head," as if that's news to her. "Feelings are foreign. Being in a relationship with me would be like teaching Emotion 101."

"I know," she agrees. "And I'm not certain I'm ready for that. I like you. I'm delighted that you're willing to look at yourself and change. But. . . ."

I lean back and we sit beside each other, motionless.

Eventually I turn towards her, but she's staring blankly and doesn't look at me. I return my gaze to the ocean.

"Maybe I should leave for awhile and give us some time to think things over. I could continue my journey to California or go back to Pennsylvania," hoping these suggestions will be rejected.

No response. A long period of silence.

Finally she says, "I have to go."

"Stay. Please. Let's sit here till morning. . . I don't want to go away."

"Then don't," she says.

She gets quiet again. This time I let the matter rest.

"Well, Alan," she says firmly, "I must go."

Reluctantly I agree. I don't look at my watch, but I know it's late. If I looked, I'd fall asleep. We walk back to the house and she opens the car door.

"Goodnight," she says, and gives me a kiss. "I'm sorry."

"Goodnight, Jean." There seems to be a note of finality and sadness in my voice.

34.

I trudge into the apartment and look at the clock. 11:45 P.M. This isn't exactly the schedule to keep in order to get up early.

At 5:00 A.M. the alarm goes off and I literally crawl out of bed. I do some half-hearted yoga and go back to bed instead of meditating. I sleep until seven-thirty. I sit up in bed and wedge the pillow behind my back. Thoughts tumble out. Should I stay? Should I go to California? Should I go back to Pennsylvania? I can find reasons to support any of these choices. For about an hour I play with the possibilities, even rehearsing conversations with people and providing their responses. Eventually I get up without having made a decision.

After breakfast I open the door to see what the day looks like. It looks like a day—sun, sky, clouds, grass. I guess I expected more. I close the door before realizing that Mrs. Crawley is sitting on the porch, so I open it again and say good morning. That's followed by "I'm returning to Pennsylvania."

She looks surprised. "You are?"

I'm surprised too but inform her that I have to attend to some old business.

"Really?" she questions.

Unable to lie I correct myself. "No. That's not true. I'm not sure why I'm going." After that words flow as if a dam broke. "Last night I wanted to tell Jean that I thought I loved her, and it didn't go well. She's uncertain about a relationship because, well, because of me. I think she thinks I think too much."

Mrs. Crawley chuckles.

"So," I continue, "I thought about it this morning and was looking at the possibilities. But just now I made the decision. First I'm returning to Pennsylvania and then I might head for California, the right way."

"You could go," she says.

"I know and I just might."

"Tell me again why you'd go to California."

"I'm not sure anymore. Originally I thought I'd ride my motorcycle there and find enlightenment on the way. Instead I ended up here which might have been a detour."

"I don't believe in detours," she says, rocking gently in her chair.

I sit down on the step, lean against the post, and ponder her comment. Finally I ask, "Why?"

"Because that's like saying there's only one route or one destination where you have to go. I don't see life that way."

"Why?"

"I believe all possibilities exist. For instance, you could stay here if you wanted or you could go to Pennsylvania or California. You could be with Jean today or never see her again. You could help me with the center. There are many opportunities available and you're going to choose the one you want."

"I see what you mean. But, how do I know which is the 'right' one?"

"What do you mean by the right one?"

"The one that will . . . I don't know . . . keep life flowing peacefully and calmly."

"And which one of your choices will do that?" Mrs. Crawley asks.

"I don't know. That's where I'm confused."

"Well, maybe you could look at it this way. Is it possible for you to be peaceful in New Jersey?"

"Sure."

"Pennsylvania?"

"Yeah."

California?"

"Probably."

"What makes the difference?"

I consider momentarily and say, "I guess the events that happen to me while I'm there."

"Or," Mrs. Crawley suggests, "is it how you respond to those events?"

"Well, yeah. I suppose that's true."

"So it's not the place or the events that make the difference?"

I can't help but smile and laugh at myself. "No, it's me. I can choose to be peaceful or not."

Mrs. Crawley laughs too. "Stuart always said to lighten up," she remembers. "'It's not what we choose to do but who we choose to be,' he used to say."

"I'm really sorry that I didn't get to meet him."

"Yes," she sighs. "But he's still helping."

I stand up to leave. "Thank you, Mrs. Crawley. I'll try to keep our conversation in mind while I'm gone."

"I hope you decide to come back. You've spoiled me,

you know. I might not get another gardener like you. Especially one who weeds so well."

I walk back into my apartment so I can call Jean at the office and tell her my plans. She doesn't seem surprised which doesn't surprise me either. We arrange dinner for tomorrow night.

I head for the beach and a late-morning stroll. After taking off my shoes I walk on the wet sand just out of the ocean's reach, postviewing the events of the last several days as well as my conversation with Mrs. Crawley. Questions rumble through my mind—how do I choose my attitude when most of the time I'm not even aware of what I'm doing? And to make matters worse, life just seems to bring one problem after another. I don't understand.

Suddenly that voice, which is maybe me, says, "Nothing in your life happens that you haven't attracted or allowed in some way."

"What do you mean?" I say to myself.

"Your outer world reflects your inner world."

I don't like that answer. That would mean, in a sense, that not only am I responsible for my attitude but also for everything that happens in my life. I walk and ponder. Is it possible that I attract the events in my life? If thoughts are energy, could they actually function like a magnet? Could my unconscious and conscious thoughts determine what I experience?

I'm not sure I want to accept all this responsibility.

35.

The rest of Thursday and almost all of Friday disappear. It's now time for dinner with Jean and I both anticipate and fear this event. It might be the last time I see her. This thought worries me.

Jean picks me up at six on the dot, not six-ish, and her punctuality worries me.

There's an uneasiness about the whole thing but she seems relaxed. She doesn't ask where I want to eat but just starts driving.

"Are you nervous?" she asks.

"Very," I say.

"Why?"

"I don't know what's going on. I really don't want to leave, but tomorrow I'm leaving. I like to know what I'm doing ahead of time."

"I see," she says, "and do you ever?"

"Do I ever what?" I ask.

"Know things ahead of time."

"Sure," I say and wonder why she asked the question. "Most of the time."

"Did you know you were coming to Ocean City?"

"Not really."

"Did you know you were going to meet me?"

"No."

"Do you know what's going to happen tonight?"

"Of course, we're going out to dinner."

She swerves the car to the right toward a telephone pole. "Nope," she says. "We just hit that pole and were killed."

I gasp. "What are you doing?"

"Just demonstrating a point," Jean says as calmly as if we hadn't come within a few feet of hitting a pole.

"Next time tell me, don't show me."

"Okay," she agrees.

"I think my life flashed before my eyes."

"How did that feel?"

"Scary. I hope I have time to improve the quality."

Jean smiles and nonchalantly continues driving.

"What was your point?"

"Just to demonstrate that we don't know what's going to happen next," she says. "If you breathe out and don't breathe in, this life as you know it is over. Do you know when you're going to take that last breath?"

"Actually, I thought it was about twenty telephone poles ago."

"That wasn't even close."

"That depends on which side of the car you're sitting in," I insist.

We drive a few miles as I reflect on this unusual start to our evening. Finally, "So you're saying that life just happens and one minute I'm alive and the next one dead?"

"Well, Alan, I can't speak for you, but I know I'm not at a place where I can see the future. I believe I influence it somehow, but I'm as surprised as anyone by the way it unfolds. So I try to be present in the moment and live according to my highest ideals. And then when I die, I'll know I did the best I could."

"That's an interesting philosophy."

I drift off into thought until we arrive at the restaurant. We pull into a parking lot on the bay. Tucked behind some older buildings is a little restaurant overlooking the water. The hostess seats us on the outside deck where we can see the docked boats.

After we place our order Jean looks up and says, "So, what are you thinking now?"

"About the fact that I could be dead any second."

She leans her head on her hand. "I wasn't suggesting that you start worrying about it. I was hoping to show you that it's more important to live in the moment and not fret about the future."

"I suppose this has something to do with 'being'?"

"A little," Jean says.

Our meals arrive and we rearrange the platters. I give her my mushrooms and she replaces them with broccoli. The meal is delicious. After the table is cleared, we linger and look over the bay.

"I wonder what the future holds," I ask rhetorically.

"Don't try to figure it out, Alan. Just be and that will influence what happens."

After a long period of silence, more than usual, Jean says, "I have one request."

"Anything," is my quick response.

"Would you print out your book and let Alice and me read it while you're gone? And, if you don't return, just ask for it and we'll send it to you."

I'm delighted they want to read my book and sad that she apparently thinks it's a real possibility I might not return. "Sure," I say. "I'll leave it on the kitchen table."

I wish I could stretch this evening into eternity, but

evening is not eternity and it comes to an end. Jean drops me off, kisses me, and says goodbye. She seems neither happy nor sad. Just accepting.

I, on the other hand, am sad. "Goodbye, Jean," I say. "Thanks for everything. I hope to see you soon."

Her eyes tell me, stop worrying.

36.

Morning comes quickly. I yoga (can that be a verb?) and meditate at five A.M., then have a quick breakfast. I put on a long sleeve shirt and jacket, knowing Jean would laugh at me.

"Almost winter," she'd comment.

"Yeah, probably sixty-eight degrees," I'd tell her.

I glance around the house taking one last look. My book is neatly stacked on the table. I wonder if they'll like it, but I have other matters to think about so I don't dwell on the subject. It's time to go.

As I pack the cycle I review what I'm taking with me: clothes, computer, Walkman, tapes and a few books. Directions are securely taped on the tachometer. I kick start the cycle and I'm off. Except for a few small trips with Jean, I haven't ridden the motorcycle much. I'm already worried that I'll get cramps. I look at the gas gauge and see that I need gas. That will give me an opportunity to stop soon which will probably coincide with my first cramp.

I concentrate while driving through the traffic circle so I come out on the right road. I try to picture the upcoming scenery but to no avail. My sense of direction hasn't improved during my stay in New Jersey.

A question goes through my mind. If I don't go back, what possessions will I give up? I picture the books, steamer, telephone, printer, some clothes and a few other odds and ends. Not too major. I wonder to myself why I'm having these thoughts.

"Whoa," I yell as a cramp sets in. I look ahead and see the sign for a gas station. A block later I leap off the cycle so I can stretch my leg. The cramp slowly eases. Now I worry about whether the cap will stick or if I'll spill gas. Neither happens so I worried for nothing. I know the cycle can make it the rest of the way on this tank of gas but I wonder if I can. I don't check for my wallet because I know it's there.

The more I ride, the more I notice the same pleasant experience that I felt on the way to New Jersey. I relax and feel peaceful. I don't experience any more cramps. Soon I pass the dairy but don't stop. Normally I would get a milkshake on the way home to Pennsylvania, but I realize it would be difficult to drink and drive a cycle. Next I approach the four-lane section of highway leading to the bridge.

I go around the curve, down the ramp, head for the bridge, and panic. I may have changed a lot, but I haven't changed a *lot*. I still worry about falling off the cycle at the top of the bridge and tumbling into the water. The thought sends chills through me. I guess I really am afraid of dying. Why do I think these things? My thought boxes are filled with strange imaginings.

I cross the bridge safely and stop to pay the toll. While I stuff the change into my right pocket, my left hand slips off the clutch and I depart faster than expected.

Half way home. New Jersey thoughts fade and Pennsylvania ones emerge. Where will I stay? I wonder if Emily or Mark will be home. I wonder how my businesses are doing. My former businesses. It feels strange going home. A half a year has passed. Is this home anymore? I think about riding to California. Why not? I think about Jean and that's my answer.

I realize the closer I get to Pennsylvania, the more I start thinking about the past. Apparently, and this is just a guess, the robot portion of me can be quickly activated by familiar surroundings. And it does make sense since there are more similar thoughts in the thought boxes. I drive through a small town in Delaware and realize there are twenty-five years' worth of thoughts about it in the thought box. That means there are forty-two years' worth of thoughts about Pennsylvania.

More familiar territory automatically starts thoughts, fears and even some anger about Sheila. Amazing. I don't have any control over these thoughts and feelings. They're tumbling out. I'll try to observe them and not react.

I hear Jean, "Don't try, just be."

"Okay," I say, pondering whether she heard me or not.

The cycle drives itself to the same motel I stayed in after the separation with Sheila. I'm back. Now what?

As I check-in, I begin worrying about money. One week in the motel will cost about a half-month's rent at Mrs. Crawley's. This is going to be expensive so I sure hope there's a purpose in my being here. I unpack the cycle. My first thought is to call Jean and tell her I arrived safely. My second thought's the same so I call even though I'm nervous. Our conversation is brief. We're probably both wondering what I'm doing here. I detect my short and shallow breathing.

I unpack my few possessions and sit on the bed. Staring at the wall makes me sleepy but I know it's only early afternoon. I force myself to get up, change clothes and go out. I decide to eat and remember a Chinese restaurant where Sheila always wanted to go. I refused then but I can't recall why. I suppose it was because I was expected to mix rice and vegetables. Anyway, times change and the meal is good. Early afternoon. What now? I decide to visit my store. Fred's store, I correct myself.

37.

I park the cycle and walk into my former business.

"Hey, look who's here," Fred says loudly enough so that a few customers hear him. "Where have you been? Someone said you went to California."

"I'm fine. I was in New Jersey."

"On the beach with the babes, right?"

"Not quite," but I smile at the thought.

"Start any new businesses?"

"No, I was taking some time off to think. Nothing exciting. But how about you? How's the new owner of this thriving business?"

"The store's been doing great," he says. "You're going to be sorry you ever sold it."

"I don't think so." Standing here talking to Fred makes me very conscious of the phrase, "a fish out of water." I look at the merchandise: cards, crafts, gift items. How did I ask my employees to sell these things to customers? Even though I only did the accounting, what was I doing in this business? What am I doing here now?

Fred is eager to take me on a tour and show me everything that's new. I go reluctantly and comment as positively as I can. He's so friendly that everyone likes him and I can understand why business is doing well.

We return to the front counter, and he motions for me to step behind it where I see an elaborate alarm system. "We had this put in a few months ago. There were a lot of burglaries in the area and I got concerned."

I nod as if comprehending, but my thoughts are elsewhere. Business, profits and loss, new merchandise, stealing. I'm suffocating in the store. "That's . . . ah." I can't find any words. "Protective."

"Yeah," he says. "It's a shame but I didn't know what else to do."

I glance at my watch and tell Fred, "Hey, I didn't realize how late it was. I have to get going. It was good seeing you again."

"Are you back to stay?"

"No, just for awhile," I tell him and feel certain about this statement.

"Well, if I don't see you again, take care."

Outside I gulp air. I know it's an overreaction to the situation but I don't know how I ran the gift shop. I bought merchandise at a lower price so I could sell it at a higher price to customers who had to be talked into buying it. For the most part, they didn't need it. In order to buy what I had to sell, they had to make money from someone else. And this someone else had to do the same thing. That's how we live. That's how people have jobs. That's how I went to New Jersey. I sit on the cycle.

I know Fred's looking out the window and probably wondering if something's wrong. He's a caring person. I start the engine, turn back, wave and drive off. I enjoyed seeing Fred. Because he bought the store from me and is selling merchandise to make a living doesn't make him good or bad. I realize I wasn't reacting to him, I was seeing a part of me with which I could no longer identify. It was like a snake that had shed its skin. When it was my skin, it was helpful. Now that I've shed it, I don't want it back. Lesson one.

On the way back to the motel I consider stopping for dinner but decide against it. Right now I only want to return to my room. I learned an important lesson. Whatever work I do in the future has to have meaning and purpose for me as well as others. I breathe easier. "Right Livelihood," Buddha called it.

Back at the motel I want to call Mark and Emily but I doubt if they're home. If they aren't, Sheila will answer and I know I'm not ready to talk to her. I consider the possibilities and finally pick up the phone and dial. Sheila answers. I don't talk. She says hello a second time.

"Hello, Sheila. This is Alan," I finally mumble.

Now she hesitates. She's probably thinking, what does *he* want?

The pause seems endless.

Finally, "Hello, Alan."

"Are Emily and Mark there?" I ask with an audible strain in my voice.

"No," she answers and doesn't offer any more information.

"Will they be there soon?" I ask, remembering how getting a response was difficult.

"No," she answers.

Frustration. "When will they be home? Tomorrow, the next day, next week?"

I hear her sigh. He hasn't changed a bit, she's thinking to herself.

"They won't be here for awhile. They come and go as they please. You just disappeared. No one knew where you were for a long time."

Guilt. "I needed some time to put my life back together."

She doesn't speak.

"Tell them I said hello. I'll probably be leaving again soon. Goodbye." I hang up before she can respond. My head is swirling. She activates every thought in the thought box and I react to every single one. I lie back on the bed. Honestly, the room is spinning. "Toto," I say, "We're not in New Jersey anymore." I hold on to the sides of the bed to keep from falling off.

"Lesson two," I say.

"What did I learn?"

"Don't call Sheila again."

Rerun lesson two.

38.

After a few minutes the room—or my head—stops spinning. I need to meditate, or do something, so I sit on the floor, or rather collapse onto the floor, pull myself into a semi-semi lotus position and wait. My mind darts in every direction. Call Jean. Call Sheila again. Get dinner. Go to the movies. Turn on a tape. Thoughts are traveling rapidly.

Alan 2? Are you here?

No one answers. But maybe he's here and I'm not since my mind is so busy and noisy. I probably couldn't hear him anyway. That's a good possibility. He's calling but getting a busy signal. Or, maybe he just stayed in New Jersey. I slow my breath to a more controlled pattern. I count breaths and barely get to three as my mind continually replays that brief, uncomfortable conversation with Sheila.

I concentrate on breathing and feel my shoulders begin to relax. They had been lodged somewhere near my ears. Even my feet are feeling better. Rhythmic breathing continues by itself. I'm sort of riding the breaths, like sitting on a surfboard in the ocean and riding the waves before they break. I'm counting and not counting and breathing and not breathing. A calmness pervades the room. Tension melts away.

I have a strange feeling that I'm watching the events of the day from a different perspective. It's certainly not Alan 1's. Maybe it's Alan 2's or 3's. I can tell this perspective has a better view of the situation than I did. I'm seeing it, but I'm not running after it. It's more panoramic. I'm reviewing it, sort of, but not like I postview conversations. I'm evaluating what I did but not condemning it. I understand Alan 1's thoughts and feelings, and I feel compassion for Sheila. I don't want either one of us to hurt or suffer. I'm above and reaching down to comfort her with the same balm that's healing me.

The feeling dissolves. Now I'm nowhere. I know I'm breathing, but it feels like a machine doing it mechanically. It's a strange sensation. I'm not thinking the way I usually do, but there is thought. I feel . . . "up here." There's no other way to describe it. And down there, Earth, seems far way. The beach and shore, the motorcycle ride back, conversations with Fred and Sheila seem . . . less intense. This is such an expansive feeling. I believe I could sit here for centuries without moving.

Something triggers an end to this sensation. Maybe it was a question about myself, like *where* am I or *who* am I. I don't know that for certain. I'm conscious of my body again and wiggle my toes to make sure they're here. They are. I take a deep breath and my chest moves. I blink and open my eyes. The room comes back into focus. I move my neck slowly.

I've heard people talk about out-of-body experiences, but I wasn't out of my body. It wasn't like I went out and left an empty shell for someone else to crawl into while I was gone. I felt I was all three Alans at once.

I know one thing for certain. From that broader, expanded perspective, I didn't have any animosity toward Sheila. In fact, I only felt compassion and wanted to help her.

In terms of views, the world from Alan 1's perspective is very limited. It's like watching a ballgame through a hole cut in a wooden fence. But, amazingly, I know that I'm the one who chooses this perspective. This reminds me of appointments with the optometrist when he tries new lenses on me and says, "Better with one or better with two?" Looking at life through Alan 1's view is like answering, "Number one is better because I'm used to it even though it's blurry and distorted. If I select lens number two, I'll have to change. I'll stay with number one."

Change is difficult and easy. It's difficult because habits are hard to break. They're the beliefs and behaviors by which I've lived. But it's easy when I finally see that they're binding and restrictive. Apparently I'm going to have to strip away the boundaries one at a time. And just because I'm at one step doesn't mean Sheila is at the same one. What do we have in common? Maybe we can concentrate on the similarities instead of the differences.

"Common ground," I say aloud as the words form in my head, "will be the vehicle to change my life. Common ground." But, I have no idea what that idea means. It just came out of my mouth.

39.

The movie *Flatliners* is on the cable channel. At nine P.M. I'm propped up in bed with a box of crackers and a soda within reaching distance. When I watch television and become engrossed in a movie or excited over a tennis match, the "robot me" eats too much. The "aware me" eventually moves the food just out of reach. Alan's Law: if you can't reach it, you can't eat it.

Anyway, the movie is about a group of medical students who decide to experiment with stopping their hearts and, after a predetermined amount of time, starting them again with electric shocks. They do this in order to experience a near-death state which they are able to recall when they return to life.

I get so involved in the drama I devour the crackers before I can get them out of reach. When the movie ends, I'm left wondering about death. I know my physical body dies, but do my emotions and thoughts continue? The medical students had individual experiences during their near-death states in which they reviewed portions of their lives. Is that right? Would I really review my life?

I try to meditate with these questions in mind. After a few minutes I feel myself relaxing, shoulders dropping, breathing deepening and calming. Thoughts about death start flowing.

Motorcycle Enlightenment

Death is an opportunity to review life. All thoughts, words and deeds are stored according to their vibrations and intensities and are available to be read like a journal. Although my physical body no longer exists, there is a part of me that observes the life I just lived. I can experience the thoughts and feelings of each past moment. If I have a lot of unkind thoughts and feelings, I probably won't be pleased with myself. I'll probably want to make amends immediately but, being dead, I won't be able to.

This realization startles me, and my awareness shifts back to the motel room. I like the idea of reading a death journal. I can imagine myself reviewing the entries and wondering why I wasted my life doing such stupid things.

I hear a voice say "Wait!" so I wait. Nothing happens. Slowly I start to visualize pleasant memories. Of course. This is another pattern of mine. I judge myself harshly. Not everything I've done has been inconsiderate. Along the way I have been kind. Maybe not as much as I wish now.

I think of Sheila, Mark and Emily and recall wonderful times. I remember pushing the children on the swings, playing baseball and tennis, and riding bicycles with them. I picture myself helping Sheila tuck the kids into bed and kissing them goodnight. I recall some great moments laughing with her. These too will be included in my review.

This also sheds new light on my idea of "being" because, remembering Jean's lesson about the telephone pole, I realize I don't know if I have one breath or fifty years' worth left. I'd rather make amends here and now than spend my time in death fretting over "mistakes" that I could have corrected while I was here.

Another memory comes to me of the story about the

knight. When I was asleep inside my armor, I mechanically went through the motions of living. But now that I'm a little more awake than I was, I can emerge from my protective shell and begin choosing who I want to be. I can decide who Alan is and how he's going to live in the world.

Maybe there is hope that Alan 1 and Alan 2 can live together harmoniously and become Alan 3. I can almost hear Alan 2 saying, "I wish he'd stop thinking we're separate people."

The 5:00 A.M. alarm startles me. I shower and dress so I won't fall asleep during yoga and meditation. Refreshed, I sit in my semi-semi lotus position waiting for new insights. Nothing happens. Around seven I straighten my legs and stand up. I have nowhere to go and nothing to do.

I walk around the room several times and finally sit on the bed. I wonder if I returned to Pennsylvania for the information I received last night. Maybe the situation with Sheila combined with the movie triggered it. Looking at life as if I've already died puts a whole new light on things. I would like to improve the quality of my life before I read it in my death journal. The amazing fact is that I can start *now*. I can choose who and how I want to be.

I get excited about the upcoming day. What will I learn? What will happen at breakfast? What will I do? Where will I go? What event will be the catalyst for a breakthrough in understanding?

The sound of a tuning fork vibrates in my head. I'm not sure if it's a C or E. The vibration conveys a message: "Nothing happens by coincidence. You can learn from everything, every moment. Being is continuous enlightenment."

40.

I head out for breakfast. As I ride my motorcycle, I think about the notion that there are no coincidences. Does everything appear for a reason? I decide to look at each event with a new perspective. Instead of dredging up all the thoughts in the thought boxes, I want to look at things fresh. I pretend I'm opening my eyes for the first time and have to make sense out of whatever is in front of me. I pull into the restaurant parking lot. Normally I would think, this is the restaurant where Sheila and I ate many times. She would get this and I would get that. On and on the thoughts would go. But, today, I pull into the parking lot as if I've never been here before.

I look at the people in the restaurant and notice that very few appear to be happy. They must be looking at life through their habits and patterns, through their walls and boundaries. I want to tap them on the shoulder and say, "Look at yourself. Are you the person you want to be? If not, change." I try to send the message through thought waves. Some people look at me. I wonder if they're getting the message. Then I realize they're probably looking at me because I'm smiling so much. I can't contain this feeling of joy. How could eating breakfast by myself in a restaurant where Sheila and I used to eat be joyful?

Beyond me. I can almost hear Alan 2 laughing. "That's right. Get out of yourself and the world takes on a whole new dimension."

I walk out to the motorcycle. My first impulse is to drive over to my former house and share these insights with Sheila. But two more thoughts occur to me. One is that this buoyant feeling is temporary. Two is that Sheila would think I'm crazy. In fact, talking to her might snap me back into my old habits just like Jean's analogy of the rubber bands.

Instead I ride to a park.

I sit and stare at the lake even though there aren't any waves. Water is water. The day is peaceful and calm. Time passes and soon it's time for a late lunch or an early dinner. I drive to a restaurant, eat an ordinary meal, and return to the motel. Nothing spectacular.

Honestly, I had hoped for a little more, like some major event, maybe even the sky opening up with a thundering voice saying, "Alan, you are enlightened." But, I suppose enlightenment is one breath at a time. When I look for it *out there,* I'm missing it every moment *in here,* between the inhalation and exhalation. Breathe in. Breathe out. There: that's enlightenment.

At the motel room I look at the movie guide to plan my evening. Tonight I'll watch the movie *Ghost.* I wonder if Alan 2 programmed the cable channel this week.

This time I'm better prepared with a double snack. Propped up in bed with popcorn and soda within reach, I become involved in the movie.

Prompted by the film I wonder if death has several levels, and if the lower ones are much like life here on Earth, except that I'd be without a body. If the universe is essence at different vibrations, then "death" interpenetrates "life" but at a different frequency. One day I'm alive and the wall in front of me seems thick and real. The next day I'm dead and I walk through it.

The desires and attachments I have when I'm alive are the desires and attachments I have when I'm dead. At death I might shed the physical layers of the Alans and look at all my thoughts, words and deeds from the all-pervasive, all-knowing, limitless, incomprehensible essence. When I see how I lived my life, I might hit myself on my head (if I still have one) and say, "What were you doing?"

I reach into an empty bag. Alan's Law: When the popcorn's gone, it's time for bed.

41.

I sleep until the alarm goes off at five, at which time I awaken and try to remember when I went to bed. This, I figure, will help me determine if I had enough sleep or not. But since I'm not certain exactly when I went to bed, I don't know if I slept five or eight hours. Consequently, I don't know whether I should still be tired or not.

I think I'd like to live without a clock, on an experimental basis. What if I lived on "ish" time? Eat when I'm hungry and sleep when I'm tired. The rising and setting of the sun would be a gauge, but that would only keep matters within an eight or twelve hour range. The rest would be hit or miss. I can hear Jean's disbelief, "You, Alan Pierce, the person whom the authorities call to check the accuracy of Greenwich Mean Time, are going clockless?"

I can't, however, pursue this idea any further now. It's five and I have to meditate. I sit for an hour, count breaths, think, and occasionally yawn. I end up going back to bed for awhile because I don't have anything else to do.

The weather is damp; in fact, the motorcycle is wet with dew. The thought of a warm, dry car passes through my mind. But for now, I kickstart the cycle and wait for it to warm up.

Motorcycle Enlightenment

I'm not sure why, but I head for the university, where I earned my degrees, and eat breakfast at the local diner. I decide to visit the library and look at my thesis housed in the poetry section. After reading it I reflect on the person I was when I wrote it. That Alan and this Alan, twenty-some years later, are different people. In a sense, I emerged from him, through a sort of transformation.

I explore the new section of the library and discover what appears to be a living room. I notice a comfortable chair overlooking the lake and know that I'll be here for awhile.

Probably an hour or more passes before I rouse myself to walk over to the book shelves. I skim the titles, pull some books off, flip through the pages and put them back. I don't feel inclined to read at the moment. Eventually I return to a seat by the window.

I gaze about the room until my eyes stop at a painting that I didn't see before. It's a still life in which one side of a bowl is filled with apples and the other side with oranges. But the fruit in the middle is a composite of apples and oranges as the transition is made from one side of the bowl to the other. Clever idea.

Suddenly there's a burst of understanding. Without my computer handy it's difficult to remember and record the information. I try to trace it step by step and make some notes. In these brief expansions life seems so clear. It goes something like this: Most of the time we believe that we are this body with its thoughts and emotions, constricted and confined by our fears and anxieties. We are apples and only apples. But, somehow, we feel intuitively that we are oranges too, a limitless energy. And maybe life is harmonious and balanced when we accept our being as the composite fruit in the middle, apples *and* oranges, outer self and inner self.

I put down my notebook and lean back. A few minutes later I take off my shoes and relax a little more. I feel like I'm back home in New Jersey. Soon I'm sleeping.

I'm awakened by two students discussing where they plan to eat dinner. Dinner? What about lunch? Where has the day gone? I better get moving if I want to eat in the dining hall. I go downstairs, cross the campus and head for the old, familiar building. I go through the cafeteria line, recalling many former meals, and wait to pay the cashier. I'm astonished to see a bowl of apples and oranges sitting beside the register. I pick up the one in the middle to see if it's a combination fruit and stare intently. The cashier is waiting. The person in line behind me clears his throat impatiently. He says abruptly, "Are you taking it or not?"

"Yes," I say. "I'm taking the apple."

"Orange," he responds with irritation. "You have an orange!"

I pay for my meal, find an empty table and eat by myself, just like old times. Afterwards I head for the bookstore to buy my evening snacks.

Back at the motel I turn on the television and use the remote to search for something interesting. I used to watch anything that came on just for something to do. This evening I turn off the television.

I get out the computer and decide to type a brief summary of my trip to Pennsylvania. I try to recall where I've been and what I've done. Sometimes I can even remember what I was thinking or feeling at certain times. Looking at life with this perspective leads me to the realization that each day is a mini-death.

42.

5:00 A.M. comes quickly. Well, actually, it comes at 5:00 A.M. Quickly is my perception. I yoga, meditate, shower and dress. Stepping outside into a drizzle makes me wish I had a car. Soon it will be colder and what then? If I wear long sleeve shirts and freeze in the summer, what will I do in winter?

I like and don't like the motorcycle. Lately I've been more afraid of it because I sometimes picture myself falling off and body surfing along the road.

The drizzle stops and I go out and start the cycle. While it's warming up, I wipe off the seat and think about the last few days. I may not have assimilated all the information, but it has changed me. I have a new perspective on life. One thing I know for certain, Alan 1 and his boundaries cause a lot of suffering for myself and others. Amazingly, an expanded, broader vision is available to me anytime I'm ready.

The cycle roars at 5000 RPMs, so I turn off the choke and put it in gear. It occurs to me that I have no idea where I'm going. That's not unusual by itself, but usually I have a destination in mind and get lost in the process. This morning I don't have a destination so I can't get lost.

I turn right and then left, on an experimental basis. Suddenly I discover I'm headed towards what I must now call Sheila's house. I want to say "my house" but refrain. I'd like to see Mark and Emily, but I'm not ready to talk with Sheila again. I turn on to the street.

There's Sheila. Apparently she and her dog have just returned from a walk. The dog is new and doesn't know me, so he watches me approach. Sheila knows me and my cycle-riding ability and quickly steps up on the curb, pulling the dog with her. I stop and take off my helmet. She doesn't appear excited to see me.

"Hello," she says coldly.

"Hello," I answer. "How are you?"

"Fine," she responds.

Long pause.

"Are Mark and Emily home?"

"No."

Long pause, swallow a few times.

"Where are they?"

"Away."

"Will they be home soon?" I continue, piece by piece.

"No, I told you on the phone. They won't be back for a while. I'm never sure where they're going and when they're coming back."

Several unkind thoughts almost become words, but I pause and stop them. Instead I say, "Well, they always have been rather independent."

"Yes," she agrees. "They like their freedom and neither one wants to be tied down with a permanent job right away." I detect concern in her voice. "They have your wanderlust."

"My wanderlust?" I say and watch for an expression.

Motorcycle Enlightenment

She half-smiles so I continue. "Just because I don't have a job, house or car. You call that wanderlust?"

"Yeah, I think that's what I mean."

A wall of separation weakens.

I recall my evening meditation in which I felt the healing balm and wanted to help Sheila. "How are you really?" I ask.

"Honestly, it's been difficult at times. But, all in all, I'm fine." She starts to say something and stops. She starts again, "Did you find your happiness? I mean, are you happy, Alan?"

I sigh. I don't know how to answer. I can't tell her about the changes. To her, the exterior is the same old Alan. And, since our divorce, I haven't done much to show Sheila that the interior is slowly changing. Besides, she's practical. You get up and go to work. You do the best you can. You don't question life. Cause and effect exist. Put your finger in the steamer and it gets burned.

Finally I answer. "Yes, in a way, I'm happy, Sheila. I've discovered something extremely important. Happiness is not to be found 'out there.' It's inside. I was too busy looking for it somewhere else. I'm changing. A different kind of happiness is emerging."

She doesn't question this and says, "Good. I'm glad for you."

I don't want to push the exchange so I conclude, "Well, Sheila, it was nice seeing you. When you hear from Mark and Emily, please let them know I stopped by. I'll be settling down soon and maybe they can visit." I pause. "I'm sorry, Sheila. I never meant to cause you any unhappiness. I was confused. Thank you for having the courage to do what needed to be done."

She looks surprised. "Alan, I knew you were unhappy,

and I knew I couldn't answer your questions. We were both miserable and knew it. I just set us free. I did it for us. Believe me."

"I do."

We both smile awkwardly.

"Goodbye, Sheila. Take care of yourself."

43.

My stomach reminds me to eat breakfast. Actually, that's where I thought I might be going when I started out. I head for a nearby diner and go in. As I wait to be seated, I spy an acquaintance I haven't seen in awhile. My first reaction is to duck behind the hostess and sneak out before he sees me. Changing old habits is hard. My second, third and fourth thoughts are all the same, but he makes eye contact and motions for me to join him. I notice my breath, try to relax and ask the waitress to seat me at his table. He seems glad to see me.

"Well, hello, Alan," he says with enthusiasm. "It's good to see you."

"Thanks, Jack. It's nice seeing you again too. How are you doing?"

"Okay," he offers reluctantly.

"I know you a little better than that. What's wrong?"

"Holly and I were just divorced."

In an instant all this flashes through my mind. How could this be? She and Jack seemed to have everything. He was witty and fun, and she was gorgeous. I used to listen to him and look at her. It was a perfect combination.

"I'm sorry to hear that." Now what do I ask: Who

divorced whom? Where are you living? Are you still wealthy? Was it an amicable divorce? I decide on "When?"

"Just finished," he answers. "She took virtually everything."

Well, I think to myself, that eliminates are you still wealthy and was it amicable. Instead I just sit, not knowing what to say.

He continues, "Holly wanted the divorce. 'Freedom,' she said. And somehow she thought I prevented it. Before I knew it, everything was over. I have a lot of bitterness and anger."

"I'm sorry," I mutter, but my thoughts automatically leap to Holly. "How's she doing?"

"I don't know," he answers curtly, "and I don't care. All I know is that everyday I hope she gets run over by a truck."

Chills go through my body. "You don't mean that!" I say. "How would you feel if it actually happened?"

Suddenly I wish he could look through the eyes of his inner being. I wish he could see how this entry will look in his "death journal."

"Yeah," he reconsiders. "I don't really mean that." He pauses, "You're the first person who didn't agree with me and say, 'I know what you mean. I feel the same way about my ex-wife.' You looked shocked."

"I was. I am. I didn't expect you to say something like that."

"I'm just confused," he admits. "I'll get over it. Hey, enough about me. How's Sheila?"

"Sheila and I are divorced too."

"No. I can't believe it." He looks puzzled and ready to ask a question, but glances at his watch and stands up.

Motorcycle Enlightenment

I know he's late for something. "Sorry, Alan, I really have to run. I'd like to talk more. Give me a call and we can get together."

"I can't. I'm just in town for a short while. If I end up staying longer, I'll get in touch."

"Great." He starts to say something and stops. I know he wanted me to say hello to Sheila. "Take care," he says and leaves.

I sit and think about Jack and Holly. I understand his confusion and anger. It was like seeing a mirror image of myself after my divorce. But talking with him now helps me see where I am, at the beginning of a new path.

44.

I leave the restaurant and drive aimlessly. I pass a small car lot that I know is a one-person operation. I don't know the owner but he has a good reputation in the community. I pull in and look at the cars. He comes out of his office and looks at the motorcycle.

"Nice bike," he says.

"Thanks."

"How many miles are on it?"

This is a question I never thought about. I look down at the RPM dial. No odometer there. Inside the speedometer are the numbers I read off, "1471."

"Less than two thousand miles? What year is it?"

"I'm not sure," I tell him. "I'll check the owner's card." For some reason I put the owner's card and the title in the saddlebag before I left.

After handing it to him he says, "This is in great shape. If you ever want to sell it, let me know."

This might be easier than I imagined. "Actually, that's why I stopped. I'm interested in trading it for a car."

"Why?"

"I don't ride it much. A car would be more practical."

"Tell you what," he says. "I have an idea. What kind of car do you want?"

"Nothing expensive. Just something that will get me to New Jersey safely. I probably won't drive more than a thousand miles the rest of the year."

"I have the perfect car," he laughs. "Doesn't that sound like a used car salesman?"

I nod my head in agreement.

"Seriously. I really do. I bought a car for my daughter to use at college. Now she's taking courses in Europe." He pauses as if remembering a problem. "The car's automatic," he says apologetically.

"Good."

"Yeah? I thought you'd want a stick shift because of riding the cycle."

I realize the motorcycle gives an entirely different impression of me. I don't think of myself as the stereotypical biker. I'm scared of riding.

We walk over to the car and he opens the door. "It's in good shape."

"Looks nice," I agree.

He walks to the front and opens the hood. "It's a four cylinder."

I'm more impressed with the four doors but I say, "Good. What gas mileage does it get?"

"About thirty," he guesses. "My daughter drove it only a few miles this summer so I can't be sure. It's a one-owner. I know the guy who had it. Kept it nice. I can check with him if you want to know."

I shake my head.

"Look," he says, "I'd like to sell the car and I like your cycle. If you're willing, I'm sure we can work out a deal. What do you think?"

"Sounds good to me."

We go into his small office and I wait while he does

some calculations. In a few minutes he makes an offer which he says is the best he can do. I think he's telling the truth and it seems fair. I agree which means I'll have a little less money in the bank, but I'll have a car with a heater. A half hour later I'm the owner of a new, used car.

As I pull out of the lot I take one last look at the cycle. I have mixed feelings leaving it behind and mentally wish it well. I had thought that riding it to California would bring enlightenment, but now that has changed. I suppose I could drive the car to the West coast and rename the book *Car Enlightenment*. But, in reality, I know the path is an inward one and I'm the vehicle that has to travel it.

45.

I decide to test drive my new car. I go to the school where I used to teach and stop in my old parking space. I sit and reflect. If I had known then what I'm learning now, life would have been very different. Next I head for my former accounting firm. I have no desire to visit, but the same thoughts occur. I know I'm not that person anymore. With effort I'm becoming a little more conscious than I was. And if I continue, I'm going to write a better story of my life and I'm certain to enjoy reading it more after I die.

I drive and think. Each incident I encountered since I returned to Pennsylvania has deepened my understanding that I can choose who I want to be. Many thoughts and feelings flow through me and I try to observe them freely.

Eventually a thought of hunger appears and I recognize it. Now my thoughts are directed towards finding a restaurant. I see one a few blocks ahead and pull into the lot. I park the car and walk away from it backwards. It looks good, and it makes me feel lighter and safer.

Inside I sit down at the counter and order a salad. While I'm waiting I pick up a newspaper. In a section called "Grab Bag," there's a quotation from Thomas

Wolfe. "The whole conviction of my life now rests upon the belief that loneliness, far from being a rare and curious phenomenon, peculiar to myself and to a few other solitary men, is the central and inevitable fact of human existence."

The waitress brings my meal, so I put down the paper and redirect my thoughts. I focus on the food, and being aware as I eat. I can pursue the mysteries of the universe after lunch.

I drive back to the motel and decide to call Jean. I think I'm ready to go home—meaning New Jersey. I dial the number of the real estate office and ask for Jean. The receptionist puts me on hold. I count the minutes and mentally say $1.00, $2.00.

Jean picks up and says "Hello. May I help you?"

"Yes, I'd like to rent an apartment in Ocean City."

"Alan. How are you?"

"I'm fine, Jean. How are you?"

"Good. Where are you?"

"Still in Pennsylvania. But, guess what. I just traded the cycle for a car."

"Really?"

"Are you surprised?"

"A little," she answers. "But, on the other hand, it's almost winter here. The temperature this morning must have been 60 degrees. I turned on the heater in the car."

"So did I. I mean, just to test it. To see if it worked."

She laughs. "And you're doing okay?"

"Yes, I am. And, I'm returning to Ocean City tomorrow."

"Oh."

"I was hoping for more enthusiasm," I admit. "Maybe even a parade in my honor."

Motorcycle Enlightenment

"Tell me when you're coming and Alice and I will walk up and down the street waving flags in front of the house."

"Great. I'll be there about twelve-ish."

She laughs again. "Ish? Are you sure this is Alan?"

"Absolutely."

I walk to the motel office and tell them I'm leaving in the morning. I can almost see cords being cut.

I decide to visit the park where I proposed to Sheila and where I read the divorce agreement. I find a parking space, walk over to the lake, and find the same bench and sit down. I stare into the water and let my thoughts travel back through the years. I recall the anticipation and excitement with which I read a poem to Sheila, gave her an engagement ring, and asked her to marry me. I remember sitting in the same spot, twenty years later, crying as I saw my life disintegrating before me.

I'm guessing, from my new perspective, that a part of me went to sleep during those years, allowing an automaton, my patterns and habits, to take over. From there, events took charge and the robot reacted.

Sheila provided the wake-up call with a not-so-gentle boot out of the marital house. I left with confusion and anger, much of it directed at her. As I prepare to leave Pennsylvania now, I'm a little more awake and thankful for her courage, and, yes, love. She probably saved my life.

46.

This evening I go to bed early and wake up in the middle of the night because I'm excited about seeing Jean and Mrs. Crawley. In a way I wish I could leave right now, but that's impossible. It's hard enough finding my way in daylight.

Somehow I sleep a little longer. In the morning I awaken feeling alive and thankful, almost jumping out of bed to yoga and meditate. My thoughts spontaneously extend outward, feeling thankful for everything. I feel like hugging trees, even the lamps in my room.

I gather my possessions and put them in the car. After paying the motel bill I drive to the closest restaurant for breakfast. I feel friendly towards everyone there. I want to hug them. Instantly I know that I wouldn't worry about whether my right arm would go over their shoulder and my left one around their waist or how close to stand. I'd just hug them. I feel like sunshine. Looking at one man sitting at the counter reading a magazine makes me feel sad because he looks unhappy. If only this feeling of joy could be shared.

I sit down next to him. He looks up and nods.

"Hi. I'm Alan."

"Paul," he replies and goes back to reading and eating.

Motorcycle Enlightenment

Being friendly could be more difficult than I thought.

I order pancakes and stare straight ahead. What's so hard about talking to someone? I muster my courage and try again. "Do you live around here?"

"Yeah, Just off Route 30 toward York."

The Big Road I think but don't say, thankfully.

"Where are you from?" he asks.

"Sort of New Jersey. I lived here most of my life but I recently moved. I just came back to visit for a few days."

He nods, takes another bite and goes back to reading the article which I can see is about antiques. Previously I would have seen it, known instantly that we didn't have anything in common, and hoped my meal would arrive quickly. But today I try a different tack. "Do you collect antiques?"

"I used to." He pauses. "My wife was the collector." He pauses longer this time. "But now she has cancer."

"That's a shame."

"It's really serious," he continues. "She probably won't make it."

"Oh. I'm sorry."

He goes back to reading, seemingly not interested in conversing further. And, I wish I hadn't prodded him into talking about what must be a difficult subject. My pancakes arrive and I eat them slowly.

Paul finishes and stands up to go. "Nice talking to you, Alan. Have a safe trip back to New Jersey."

I'm amazed. "Thanks. I hope . . . ah . . . good luck."

He actually smiles as he heads for the door. And here I thought he was annoyed because I disturbed him.

Life's becoming more interesting. Maybe Paul's response was the best he could do at that moment. His thoughts and feelings are probably focused on his wife's condition and how his life has changed. His wife, obviously, is focused on her physical body and enduring the pain.

I suppose that's how life appears on the surface. An event happens and we cope with it by way of our habits and patterns. If it makes us feel good, we're happy. If it causes suffering, we're sad. Then we wait for the next one.

But, with what I've experienced in the last several months, I think there's more to it than that. Not only do I know that we can determine who we are in each situation, a part of me now believes we are responsible for which events occur. I don't understand how the connections are made, but I'm comfortable believing our thoughts, feelings and expectations contribute more than we realize.

47.

I cross the Delaware Memorial Bridge without trepidation. It's partly because I'm in a car this time, and partly because the bridge doesn't seem so scary. About an hour and a half later I enter the loop, cross the bay bridge and see the Ocean City water tower. A few minutes later I'm pulling into the driveway.

The door opens and out comes Mrs. Crawley who greets me with a big hug.

"I'm so glad to be back," I tell her. "I know it's only been a few days but it seems like a lifetime."

She hugs tighter, lets go and pats me on the back.

Jean follows, hugs and gives me a kiss. "It's good to see you."

"Thanks. I missed you."

Mrs. Crawley gestures toward my car. "So you sold the motorcycle?"

"Yeah, I discovered I like being surrounded by a roof and four sides."

"And heat," Jean adds.

"I didn't turn it on," I protest, "since the bridge."

"You had the heat on this morning?"

"It was cold up north," I tell her.

Mrs. Crawley laughs. She doesn't know about my

body's malfunctioning thermostat. "Why don't you get your things out of the car?" she suggests.

I nod in agreement and open the back door of the car. Jean collects a few of the assorted bags. Mrs. Crawley goes back into the house.

"I actually wondered whether you'd come back," Jean admits.

"Honestly?"

"I didn't know if someday I'd get a call from California," she says candidly.

"It was a fleeting thought, especially after my first conversation with Sheila. But I realized I'd probably end up here anyway."

We take my belongings into the apartment. I glance at the steamer and smile, part of me ready to resume cooking and part of me content to keep eating in restaurants.

Jean notices and asks, "Did you miss it?"

"A little," I admit.

I go upstairs to put a few things away while Jean waits downstairs. A few minutes pass and she calls up the steps. "Are you finished? And don't come down wearing anything weird because Alice wants to ask you something."

"What's it about?" I call down the steps.

"She'll tell you."

I finish quickly and practically run down the stairs.

A few minutes later Jean, Mrs. Crawley and I are sitting at the dining room table, where there are tea and muffins. I'm not much for tea, but I sip a little to be polite. I eat the muffins because they're good and I realize I haven't eaten lunch.

It's quiet and I sense something is wrong or different.

Motorcycle Enlightenment

Finally Mrs. Crawley begins, "Jean and I read your book and enjoyed it immensely."

"Great. I'm glad."

"You've inspired us with your example."

"What example is that?" I ask naively.

"To observe ourselves and continually make changes," Jean answers.

"Thanks. That's quite a compliment. It's been . . . ah . . . a challenge. And I'm probably just starting to turn the corner."

"We understand that," Mrs. Crawley says. "It's one thing to realize that we've become creatures of habit and another to explore those patterns and change. But it also takes courage to proceed and that's the inspiration. So," she continues, "I've decided that I want to make some major changes in my life and I'd like your help."

"What can I do?"

"Do you remember the property I told you about? The one with two houses overlooking the ocean?"

"Yes . . . ."

She then pauses too long, and I feel as if I jumped on a trampoline and somehow time stopped, leaving me in mid-air waiting to come down.

"As I told you once, I'd like to purchase it to develop the center, but," she clarifies, "without your help I wouldn't know where to start. From what you've told me about your business background, I feel certain you can do it."

"That's great. I know I can."

"And," she adds, "I'd like you and Jean to live with me in the one house while we rent rooms to guests in the second one. What do you think?"

"Unbelievable."

Mrs. Crawley looks startled. "But that's probably a lot to think about having just returned. Will you think it over?"

"Of course."

We let the matter rest and they ask me about the trip to Pennsylvania. I tell them generalities but emphasize how glad I am to return. After awhile Mrs. Crawley suggests that Jean and I talk things over and get back to her later.

The idea is fascinating. I am interested in helping Mrs. Crawley, but I'm more anxious to know what Jean's thoughts and feelings are about the center, and about me. Especially the part about all of us living together in one house.

We walk over to my apartment and I settle into a chair.

Jean senses my question and begins answering it. "Alice decided she was ready. When I told her that you called and said you were returning, she was quite excited."

"Excited to see me?"

"Of course," she says, "she likes you. Who doesn't?"

I pause to consider.

"Don't think about it! It was just a comment."

48.

Jean walks toward the door and asks, "Ready for a stroll? I'll bet you missed the beach. And you're probably suffering from pizza withdrawal."

"Ah, yes, the direct route to my heart—pizza."

As we go down the walk Jean takes my hand. "So," she says, "What do you think about this idea of the center?"

"It makes me a little nervous," I admit, "but I believe it can work."

"I do too," she agrees and reconsiders the comment. "But what makes you nervous?"

"Well, there is the part about the three of us living together in one house."

She nods and waits for more explanation.

"I don't know how that would work. You and I would be together all the time. How do you feel about it?"

"I'm not sure," she confesses. "I haven't decided."

We walk a few blocks on the boardwalk and go down to the water.

"Jean, I don't know if this will make the decision easier or not, but I want you to know that I really missed you."

She stops walking and turns toward me. "I missed you too."

I let out a deep sigh, thankful for that response.

"So, what do we do?" I wonder.

"Well . . . ," she slowly forms the word and stops. Long pause. "I've been doing a lot of thinking and I've made some discoveries about myself."

"Like what?"

"You've been trying hard to make changes and I've been hesitant to do the same. It was easy to see the limitations you placed on yourself while ignoring mine. And you've been very understanding of that and I've appreciated it. You're okay."

"That's it. I'm okay? You mean I pass inspection?"

She laughs, embarrassed. "No, that's not what I mean. You're . . . ah . . . who you said you were when we met. You really are . . . trustworthy . . . kind. . . ."

"Loyal and obedient," I add.

She laughs again. I'm certain that she had previewed this conversation and it's not going as she expected.

"Seriously, thank you, Jean. That means a lot. And, while we're confessing, I have one too. I know you were right about the chocolate ice cream cone. Had we started a serious relationship as soon as I arrived, it would have recycled all the old issues. I may have learned a lot since we met, but I still have to experience Emotion 101. I'm willing if you are."

She doesn't answer and dashes my expectations. I sort of hoped that she would throw herself into my arms and we'd live happily ever after.

Instead she says, "I don't know."

"About?"

"You, the center, returning to my profession. All at the same time."

"That's a lot, but let's take things as they come," I

suggest, out of character for me. "You're doubtless planning to handle the real estate transaction."

"Certainly."

"And then when the center is open, you'll shift gears and counsel the people who come to rebalance and restore their lives."

"Absolutely."

"So the uncertainty is about us?"

"Yes."

"No problem. We'll just get married."

She shakes her head. "That's one thing I like about you, Alan. You're becoming flexible. Last week you considered going to California. Today you're proposing marriage."

We change direction and head back towards the boardwalk.

"So where are you really, Alan?"

"Right here," I reply.

"Seriously."

"Well, I want to be with you, Jean and I'm just starting to sort out all the reasons why. I think I love you."

"Think?" she asks, tapping me lightly on the heart.

"I love you, Jean."

After a tender, lingering kiss I step back. "I know I have a lot of inner work to do and I'm only beginning to discover who I am. You've helped me realize so much about myself. Things I never even guessed."

She squeezes my hand.

"Before I met you, I actually thought I was aware of what I was doing. Returning to Pennsylvania helped me see some of my habits and patterns more clearly. I saw who I had been and glimpsed who I could be. Maybe an inner part of me has awakened, and I'm learning to live all over again. But I can't make promises. I know I'll regress at times."

"We all do. And I will too. But I'm glad to hear this, Alan. From that first day in my office I saw *this* you. Somehow I knew the person you could be. I thought I had dealt with the same issues myself and could be of help. But in the process I discovered that I hadn't dealt with all the levels either."

"Maybe we can help each other."

We walk into Angelo's Pizza and sit at a booth. She reaches across the table and takes my hand.

"Let's be careful not to place expectations on each other," she says.

"I'll try not to. It's definitely an area of my personality that needs work."

"We'll practice together," Jean assures me.

49.

Jean and I meet with Mrs. Crawley and tell her we're eager to help with the center. She suggests that I read the journals in which Stuart described his ideas. For several weeks the three of us spend many hours discussing the project. I compile the information and write a mission statement and business plan. We agree to use the name CommonGround because the center will be a healing place where there are no dogmatic teachings. We envision a setting where people will come to experience a peaceful environment for a few days, weeks or months, coming and going as need arises.

Jean presents Mrs. Crawley's offer on the property, and it's accepted. The only contingency is that the town planning commission approve the use of the property for CommonGround. At the monthly meeting the council reviews our proposal and accepts it. Everything is ready.

For the next several months we spend our days at the house preparing it to become our new home. Jean and Mrs. Crawley are expert organizers and efficient workers. Together they accomplish the bulk of the work such as scraping and painting. I'm assigned mundane chores which don't require handyman skills—

washing windows and scrubbing floors. This isn't work that I would actually choose to do but I know it's necessary.

Since I've never done any of these things before, I find myself temporarily engaged in learning how to perform the tasks and enjoying them. Once I know how to do them with a degree of proficiency, monotony sets in and the automaton takes over.

Like right now. A part of me is getting bored washing windows so my thoughts are starting to drift. It occurs to me that this experience is similar to my first meditation with Lindy when she instructed me to concentrate on an imaginary line.

So, I force myself to focus. I spray on the window cleaner and notice how it forms droplets on the panes. I watch the mist fall slowly towards the floor. I observe the dirt in the corner beginning to dissolve. I notice the patterns formed by the cleaner and the dirt as I wipe the window with the paper towel. The process is engrossing and I finish the windows.

Mrs. Crawley startles me. "It's time to go."

Jean follows a few steps behind and sees that I'm not propped up in a corner reading a book, like I was several times previously. "I'm amazed," she admits.

"Why is that?"

"Because you're still working."

"And somewhat enjoying it?" Mrs. Crawley asks tentatively.

"Well, sort of. I'm probably more curious about how my mind and body work. The chores are getting done as a byproduct."

Mrs. Crawley sits on a chair beside me. "Alan, you're interesting. I never met anyone who had never cooked, weeded a flower bed, or washed windows. And yet you handle business matters effortlessly."

"Thank goodness I can do something."

She laughs. "Well, I'm grateful for your business skills, and I'm glad that we all have different talents and can help one another."

We collect our things and head for the truck.

Jean laughs to herself and then ventures, "Alan, speaking of skills, I wonder if you could learn to drive without getting lost all the time?"

"I doubt it."

"Seriously," she says.

"Oh, no. . . . Well, I suppose I could try. It's probably like washing windows. If I concentrate I can do it."

"We'll help you look for landmarks where you make turns," Mrs. Crawley suggests, getting excited about this experiment.

"I don't know, but let's see how it works."

Jean hands me the truck keys and slides into the middle of the seat while I climb behind the wheel. Mrs. Crawley gets in the passenger's side.

"Goodbye, CommonGround," Mrs. Crawley teases, "I hope to see you again."

"As long as one of you stays awake we'll be fine," I assure her. I turn the truck around and pull to the end of the driveway. "Which way?" I ask.

I can tell they're dumbfounded.

"What?" I ask in embarrassment.

"Alan," they say in unison, and then Jean continues, "Don't you even know which way to turn out of the driveway?"

I look left and then right. I concentrate and try to recall but nothing happens. "Right?" I guess.

Jean nods and probably suspects it was a lucky guess.

"Just remember the ocean is to your right as we go home. That means we travel north to Ocean City and south to get here. It's easy."

I picture an atlas with the Atlantic Ocean on my right. But suddenly I'm at a stop sign and don't know whether to turn or go straight. Jean sees my dismay and points out another road sign that helps orient me. Now I'm focused on learning the directions and my mind is concentrated.

"This may work," I say. "I guess I just never paid much attention to anything because I always expected someone else to do whatever needed to be done."

"I think you've made an important discovery," Mrs. Crawley says, "and that's basically that you're responsible for yourself."

"That's true," I agree. "And it all starts with observing myself carefully, discovering who I am and living accordingly."

Jean chimes in, "It's like being asleep or awake. Sleeping doesn't require effort, but being 'awake' when you're awake takes concentration."

"I enjoy conversations like this," I say.

"Me too," Jean adds, "but putting it into practice is more difficult." She taps me on my leg. "You just passed my house."

50.

The main house at CommonGround is finished. It's moving time. Mrs. Crawley, Jean and I begin hauling possessions, one small load at a time in a pickup truck that one of Mrs. Crawley's friends loans us. Helping them pack their belongings makes me glad that everything I own can fit in my car, in one trip.

The second house is not quite ready for guests and, since it required more work than the primary residence, contractors have been hired for the job. As Mrs. Crawley assured us in the beginning, money is not an issue due to the profits made from the sale of the real estate agency as well as Stuart's financial savvy.

So, we have settled into our new home and spend our days as we choose. Mrs. Crawley takes care of the domestic chores, Jean enjoys working part-time at the real estate office, and I'm responsible for handling the advertising and finances. I spend a lot of my time walking on the beach, sitting on the porch, and occasionally reading and writing in my office which overlooks the ocean. Sometimes I wander aimlessly through the house.

"What's the matter, Alan?" Jean asks.

"Nothing. Just walking around."

"Looking for something to do?"

"Depends. What do you have in mind?"

"How about finishing your book?" she suggests.

"Excellent idea," Mrs. Crawley chimes in.

I can't tell if they think the idea is good or they want me to stop pacing.

Mrs. Crawley continues, "Alan, you did everything that was needed. You guided us step by step through the process of starting this center. You organized, accounted, projected, analyzed, and theorized. You have the finances in perfect order."

"Thank you."

"You've been a tremendous help. Since Stuart died, I haven't had my checkbook balanced to the penny. And, besides, now I even know what percentage of my income is spent on vegetables."

Maybe I got a little carried away with budgeting.

I head upstairs to my office, sit down at the computer, and prepare to write. Nothing happens. In a few minutes I'm sitting in my swivel-rocker, enjoying the ocean view. There's a knock on the door.

"May I come in?" Jean asks.

"Sure."

"I won't disturb your writing?"

"Absolutely not."

I swivel the chair in her direction as she opens the door.

"At least from there you have a better view of the ocean," she says.

"I don't know what to write," I answer before she asks.

"That's why I came up. Alice and I weren't sending you away. We'd like to see your book finished. It's one of the reasons we're here at CommonGround."

I take a deep breath.

Jean walks behind me and puts her hands on my

shoulders. "Alan, I'm happy for you. I'm happy for us. When you arrived in Ocean City that first day, I saw a gentle but confused and lonesome man. Your eyes cried out for help. I remember your telling me that life seemed pointless, like trying to fill a round hole with a square peg, or something like that." She laughs. "Do you recall how nervous you were the first time we went out for dinner?"

"Yes." I smile. "All I could think about was spilling food on my slacks or getting lost coming out of the restroom. That was difficult for me."

"I know it was. And look how far you've come."

"It's all rather amazing," I agree.

Jean sits beside me on the computer chair and says, "So what's wrong?"

"I'm stuck again."

"Where?"

"Between the old me and the new me. It's become clear that all my life I've been looking for something outside of myself to make me complete and happy. I lived in a shell that reacted to life out of habits and patterns."

"And the new you?" Jean says.

"Every time I think about doing something, I wonder why I want to do it. What's the purpose? In fact, why do anything at all?"

"That's an existential question. If I recall your book correctly, that's how you felt when you crossed the Delaware Memorial Bridge. You looked at a meaningless life, and death, and chose to keep riding."

"I'm impressed that you remember my book."

"I was there, Alan, not on the bridge with you, but at a similar point where I questioned the meaning of life. What ultimately got me through was my connection with other people, and you know how important the Crawleys have been. You've avoided emotional intimacy. By thinking about life in an abstract way, you haven't allowed yourself to feel it. It's as though you've been an observer and kept people on the other side of your protective shield."

"What do you mean?"

"Maybe you view people as objects that you believe contribute to your well-being or detract from it. Because of your sense of vulnerability you keep everyone at a distance. I sometimes feel that you're most concerned with your own life being peaceful and undisturbed."

"You might be right, Jean, but I don't like seeing this quality in myself."

"Well, first you have to be aware of it before you can change it."

We sit quietly and I swivel back toward the ocean view. A few minutes pass. I swivel back toward Jean.

"There are a lot of steps to this process of changing, aren't there?"

"Yes, and we both have a lot of work to do. It's difficult to look at ourselves and find things we don't like." Jean gets up, walks over to my chair, leans down and kisses me. "But don't be too hard on yourself."

51.

Life seems so complicated at times. My breath is short and shallow. I look out the window and stare at the Atlantic, remembering all the times that I begged it for answers. Maybe they're to be found in the Pacific Ocean.

I close my eyes and breathe deeply. I do want to change. I know I can. But Jean is right. I have to observe the qualities that I don't like about myself before I can do anything about them. I tell myself I want a life of peace, love and joy, but what I mean is that I don't want anything happening that I haven't planned. I say that all people are connected, yet I distance myself from them. I anticipate those rare moments of inner peace when everything is blissful, and yet afterwards I feel there is something more, something missing. I seem to be a bundle of contradictions.

I remember asking myself earlier how I could discover the illusions I hold about myself. Then I presumed I could find all the answers in books, and they did provide an important foundation. Through philosophical explorations, meditation and careful self-observation I uncovered part of the answer as to who I am. But Jean has helped me open to an emotional component. I'm convinced there is much to be learned about who I am through relationship with others.

Previously I would have sat and pondered these notions by myself, but I go downstairs to be with Jean and Mrs. Crawley.

52.

I find them sitting on the back porch having tea.
"Care to join us?" Jean asks.
"Actually I would. Thank you."
"Writer's block?" Mrs. Crawley says.
"Human's block," I confess. "I've been trying to unravel the intricacies of life, but I shouldn't interfere with your conversation."
"I'd like to hear about it," Mrs. Crawley insists.
Jean nods in agreement.
"Well, I'm perplexed. I know I'm making some progress and changing, but each change leads to more changes. It's like a bottomless pit. And then I start wondering about the purpose of changing anyway."
"What is it that you really want?" Mrs. Crawley asks.
I consider. "To decide who I want to be and then to be that person."
"Why?" Mrs. Crawley asks again.
"That's a difficult question. Like what's my ulterior motive?"
"Okay," she agrees.
"I suppose I want my life to be meaningful."
"And how do you measure that?" she continues.
I look at Jean. "I didn't know we were living with the reincarnated Socrates."

Mrs. Crawley laughs. "Stuart and I used to have sessions like this frequently. He'd tell me about his new theory and then I'd ask questions. You don't have to answer if you're uncomfortable."

"No, it's okay. It's very clarifying. I'm just wondering how I determine if my life is meaningful. Before I met Jean I would have said, 'if everything were peaceful and I were happy.'"

"And if I recall correctly," Jean adds, "that meant you had found something that temporarily placated you."

"Right," I agree, "like the perfect chocolate ice cream cone."

Mrs. Crawley pats me on the arm. "You and Stuart would have gotten along so well."

Jean returns to the question. "So how has meeting me altered the meaning in your life?"

"Wonderfully," I say with an angelic smile.

"I mean seriously."

"Oh. Well, you know I've always been uncomfortable in the world and wanted to get through it as quickly and quietly as possible. Along the way I wanted as much peace and happiness as I could find and then I wanted to disappear. But there always seemed to be something missing."

"That's how you were feeling when you arrived in Ocean City?" Mrs. Crawley clarifies.

"Right. I was on my way to California to find that missing piece. But soon after I met Jean, she referred to the walls and barriers that I had built around myself. Then she talked about being and doing. That helped me understand how important it is to be aware of the habits and patterns which took over my life."

"And is that what you're working with now?" Mrs. Crawley wonders.

"Yes, but I know it's not the entire picture. There's more."

"Maybe this involves relationships and love. Higher connections," Jean says.

"Maybe. I haven't done well with relationships," I confess.

"Why is that?" Mrs. Crawley asks me.

"I don't know. I guess I've been too self-contained."

There's a pause in the conversation. We sip tea and Mrs. Crawley brings out some snacks.

"Alan," she says. "Let me pose a question that Stuart once asked me. It shocked me actually."

"What is it?" I ask tentatively.

"If you could choose to die right now, would you?"

"Ah . . . ah . . ." I stammer. "For most of my adult life I would probably have answered yes, I'm ready to die. But now I would say no. I want to live."

"Why is that?" she asks.

"Well, because of the survival instinct. All creatures have that, even the smallest insect, so I guess I want to live because being alive is all that I know, or at least remember."

"How about you, Jean? What is your answer?" Mrs. Crawley says.

"I definitely want to live," Jean responds. "I'm not yet the person I want to be. Sometimes this only exists as a potential, but I know it's there. But, even beyond that, I want to share my life. Maybe my words or actions can uplift or inspire others. That adds meaning and joy to my life."

"And you, Mrs. Crawley?" I ask.

"I want to live too. It doesn't matter how old a person is, there's a pull toward being better, like a higher level of being. That's my interest in CommonGround. I want to live at that higher level and share it with others. To me, that's what life and love are all about."

"This is interesting," I say. "I'm starting to see some order in the process. First I had to realize I was asleep in the world. Then I began discovering the habits and patterns that encased me. And now I'm beginning to poke my head out of the cocoon and see that others exist too."

"This is the tricky part," Mrs. Crawley says, "to see others but to know that we are all connected. Like a hologram where each part contains the whole."

"And," Jean adds, "still realizing that we all have the potential to evolve into something higher, or finer. Like a seed becoming a flower, or a caterpillar transforming into a butterfly."

"Or a human becoming more conscious," I say.

Mrs. Crawley looks delighted. "Stuart would be so happy if he were here. He envisioned CommonGround as a place where discussions like this would take place. And, even further, he hoped that people would touch this higher energy and bring it into their everyday lives to live it and share it with others. 'The ideal life,' he said, 'is allowing energy to flow unimpeded toward its potential.'"

53.

Jean and I stroll on the sand and listen to the ocean. We hold hands, hug, and kiss. These unfolding feelings must be love, and I'm aware that I want to be with Jean as we both evolve. It's exhilarating to feel the potential. It dawns on me that the only obstacle preventing me from being the person I want to be is me.

We eventually stop walking, knowing we've gone far enough. I bend down and pick up a handful of sand, letting it slip through my fingers. For once, I actually *feel* the sand. I stand up and gaze into the sky, noticing how blue it is against the wisps of white clouds. I smell the salt air. This is what I've been missing as I slept through my life.

This walk is different. Fears, anxieties, walls and barriers dissolve. I look out across the ocean before we turn inland towards CommonGround. I feel an immensity rising inside and pulling me. Maybe it's my heart opening. Maybe it's something else. I recall the voice in the night, "You are about to be taken on a journey of great proportions."

I hope it comes with directions.

About the Author

Charles Sides is a retired teacher and former owner of an insurance agency and a music store. He currently owns a health food store in Pennsylvania while writing, researching, and living in the foothills of Virginia's Blue Ridge Mountains with his wife, Jenny. *Motorcycle Enlightenment* is his first book.

Hampton Roads Publishing Company
. . . for the evolving human spirit

Hampton Roads Publishing Company
publishes books on a variety of subjects including
metaphysics, health, complementary medicine,
visionary fiction, and other related topics.

For a copy of our latest catalog,
call toll-free, 800-766-8009,
or send your name and address to:

Hampton Roads Publishing Company, Inc.
1125 Stoney Ridge Road
Charlottesville, VA 22902
e-mail: hrpc@hrpub.com
www.hrpub.com